Water
Shaper

by Laura Williams McCaffrey

Clarion Books   New York

# Acknowledgments

Thank you to Colin, Cerridwyn, and Magdalene. Without your patience and good humor, I would never finish anything. Thank you to every writer friend, for desperately calling and taking my desperate calls, as well as for reading the ridiculous e-mails I wrote when I should have been working on this story and sending me sublime e-mails in response. A tremendous thanks to this book's readers: Deb Abramson, Dale Blackwell Gasque, Anne Trooper Holbrook, Shelagh Shapiro, and Susan Ritz. Thank you to Nancy Gallt, for all her hard work and for putting up with my neurosis. And thanks to everyone at Clarion Books—with especial everlasting gratitude to Jennifer B. Greene, who demanded more than I first offered.

Clarion Books
a Houghton Mifflin Company imprint
215 Park Avenue South, New York, NY 10003
Copyright © 2006 by Laura Williams McCaffrey

The text was set in 13-point Filosofia Regular.

www.houghtonmifflinbooks.com

Printed in the U.S.A.

*Library of Congress Cataloging-in-Publication Data*

McCaffrey, Laura Williams.
Water shaper / by Laura Williams McCaffrey.
p. cm.
Summary: Having escaped from her father's control with help from a handsome holy
man who is king of a western land, fifteen-year-old Princess Margot finally travels to the
sea where her mother lived, and from which she can draw a powerful magic.
ISBN-13: 978-0-618-61489-9
ISBN-10: 0-618-61489-3
[1. Kings, queens, rulers, etc.—Fiction. 2. Magic—Fiction. 3. Water—Fiction.
4. Storytellers—Fiction. 5. Selkies—Fiction. 6. Fantasy.] I. Title.
PZ7.M122835Wat 2006
[Fic] —dc22
2005027747

QUM 10 9 8 7 6 5 4 3 2 1

*For Norman and Rebecca Williams,*
*who bear no resemblance to the parents in this book*
*and who let me read whatever and whenever I wished*

# One

argot hated feasts. The laughter was loud. The smoke from the men's pipes and the hearth's fire was thick, as was the sweaty smell from all the people pressed together: women in their tight bodices and flared skirts, men in their long tunics and greased boots. At both elbows she had lords with wind-rough, familiar faces, though if she knew them, she couldn't remember their names. They had to sit too close to her on the bench, and their trenchers touched the sides of hers on the hewn-log table. A summer shower had started as the bell rang the call to sit. She'd rather be out in it, head tilted back. She wanted to feel the raindrops running down her hair and neck. Unfortunately, she couldn't go now. Her father would notice. She didn't want to give him any reason to watch her more closely, or to suspect she was thinking of running away.

Besides that, dark had fallen and demon spirits would be prowling. They came from their secret paths, which led from their kingdom deep underground. Or they emerged out of the abandoned buildings they'd taken as their own. The walls around the town were supposed to protect it, the castle, the gardens, and the lake. People ruined bits of the wall, however, to let demon spirits in and get forbidden magics as payment. Margot watched the broadest holy man; taking care not to drip on his feasting robe, he piled his trencher high. Maybe if he and the others ate a little less, they'd be able to fix the wall more quickly.

One of the lords beside Margot started talking. "Don't you like this roast? It's very good." His sparse beard and mustache framed a smile. He started to pick at his teeth with his knife. He looked like one of the hill lords, that was why he seemed familiar. "Could I get you some more?"

He was probably a younger son who'd never left his family lands before; he didn't know who she was yet. Not another one. "I don't feel hungry," answered Margot, rudely looking at her cup instead of at him.

"Where do you think King Philip found this fine roast?" asked the lord.

*On a cow*, Margot was tempted to answer, but she didn't want to encourage him to say anything else.

"So. I bet you have to keep your fair face out of the sun," the lord went on. He didn't seem to care if she answered or not. "You must be from the northlands." He reached in front of her to grab the wine pitcher. "Would you like some more?" Without waiting for a response, he filled her glass.

Margot drummed her fingers on the table. They were as white as goat cheese, like her face and all the rest of her, except her black hair and eyes. Their paleness wasn't good for much, except maybe driving away annoying lords. "No, my mother was from the Western Isles."

The lord set down the pitcher with a thump, but instead of suddenly pretending she didn't exist, he squinted at her. "You must be the oldest daughter. The princess of this land."

*Of this land*. The words pricked hard and painful into Margot, and she wished she'd kept her mouth shut. She'd lived here all her fifteen years, but she wasn't really of this land; this land didn't want her. "I'm the king's daughter," she answered in a tone that was meant to end the conversation.

"You mean, you didn't realize you had the pleasure of sitting next to our elder princess?" asked one of Margot's cousins, Isabeau, from the lord's other side. Margot ripped the thick crust from her bread. She pretended not to notice Isabeau or the other cousins, who leaned forward to stare and giggle. She put the bread's soft center in her mouth. It was dry and tasteless.

"No, I didn't," said the lord, giving Margot a smirk.

"Why haven't you told him, Princess Margot? Especially about the queen, about who she was and where she came from?" Isabeau said, pushing her braid over her shoulder. She smiled like a cat that had got at the cream. "We'd all love to hear you talk about your mother's family."

"I'm finished." Margot rose from the bench, accidentally knocking the lord with her elbow. He bumped against Isabeau. Isabeau upset her glass. Water spilled over the table's red feast cloth and the front of Isabeau's finely woven blue dress.

"Don't you ever feel any shame? How can you use water magics in the feasting hall?" snapped Isabeau. The cousins sitting around Isabeau suddenly went silent, their perfect almond-shaped eyes all fixed on Margot. The lord shifted away from her. Margot felt her face growing splotchy red with outrage.

"I knocked into the lord," Margot retorted. "That's all I did."

The cousin nearest Isabeau shook her head, unbelieving. Suddenly, Isabeau laughed. She turned to the lord. "We can't let Princess Margot near water. Her mother was from the

Western Isles. Even the 'highest born' there are all tainted by base fortunetelling magic. They use it rather than hiding it. A strange kind of nobility, don't you think?"

The cousins started giggling again. The lord snorted. They all turned from Margot, leaving her standing alone, facing their backs. Dismissed.

Then they leaned together and started to speak of weak love potions and reading unlikely futures in water dishes, as well as fortunetellers' other pastimes. *Ignorant asses!* Margot wanted to yell.

Instead, she stalked off, pushing through a tangle of drunken lords. If she insisted that understanding water had nothing to do with fortunetelling magic, she'd only get stares and scorn. Her father would glare because she wasn't sitting quiet and drab like a rock on the ground. His present wife would give her one of those impatient sideways glances; Belinde sneered at her "base blood" but often seemed just as annoyed that Margot couldn't simply appear to obey while still doing what she wished, as Belinde herself always did. The holy men would waggle their jowls and explain that they'd tried to train her but she wouldn't learn to ignore the base magic in her blood. Others would whisper about her mother, starting off with the lie: *I don't like to speak poorly of the dead.* No one here knew anything.

Faces looked briefly at her as she passed. She didn't stop to talk. None of these people felt a thrill when the rain came down or the lake rolled and heaved in a storm. Very few had any desire to go west and stand near the greatest water of all, the Sea. If Margot hadn't found the book that had once been her mother's, she'd probably believe she *was* tainted with base magic, or had gone mad. But she was neither. She walked faster.

She broke away from the crowded tables and went to stand

in an empty corner, despite the drafts. Leaning against a wall hanging, she wished she could step back through the hanging and the stone wall, out. But she couldn't. She was shut in. She had to stay trapped with these guests, her tall, bearded father, and Belinde.

They stood together. Belinde, her belly large and round with the baby she carried, was calm and graceful as she directed scrubs with platters. She was smiling, but Margot had once overheard her say privately to the scrub she'd brought here that she missed the northern city and northern kingdom she'd come from. That land's king had been married, though, and Belinde had wanted to be a queen. Margot's father had wanted a new beautiful, well-dowered wife. So here she was. Margot had already watched her father put two wives and a daughter aside. He'd sent them to live with cousins or friends. Belinde seemed certain that even if she birthed a daughter, she wouldn't have to go. At least, if she was worried, she never showed it. Margot didn't always like Belinde, who understood nothing about water. But there were moments when the queen seemed to be trying to teach her how to always both charm and get her way. And there were moments when Margot wanted to learn from her.

Margot, however, wasn't certain Belinde *would* get her way, in the end. Though the king had given in about buying her a newer, faster horse, he probably wouldn't relent about an heir. He smiled and laughed as Belinde touched his arm, but Margot wasn't fooled. He wasn't simply enjoying himself. He was also scheming, as always, thinking of ensuring an heir and building strong alliances. His one impulsive moment, he told anyone and everyone, had been to marry Margot's mother because of her lovely eyes and hair. Neither, he let everyone know, had made up for the small dowry the Western Isle nobility had been able to afford, or the base magic in her blood. He was proud to say he'd never been impulsive again. Margot hunched when he looked her way, hiding behind large Merchant Blaas. She avoided her father when possible; unlike Belinde and the other wives, she wanted no part in his scheming.

A rhythmic clapping started. Voices shushed one another. A story, her father had called for a story. People jostled, making a wide space around the hearth for the storyteller. Margot climbed up next to Merchant Blaas's daughters, who stood on a bench. At least this would be exciting or funny. She wouldn't have to talk to anyone, and no one would talk to her.

The clapping stopped. A man walked forward to the hearth. It wasn't the storyteller who wintered here; he'd left to travel for the summer, as all of his kind did. It was another of the land's five best tale tellers, the one who wintered at the hill lords' castles. He wore his black cloak with its edging of red marnloy feathers. Underneath were his black tunic and loose trousers. He had a full beard and a homely face. He quickly crouched and leered at the crowd. A couple of small children shrieked, then laughed. He rolled his eyes and stomped his feet so that they laughed harder. Margot laughed, too. "A tale of Gwist the tricky fool, Highness?" he asked.

"My queen will choose," came Margot's father's voice. "What do you say, Belinde?"

"I'd like 'Rosalind and the Pig's Head,'" the queen answered. Margot grinned. Belinde picked good stories.

The storyteller straightened. His homely face became proud, heroic. "A very fine choice," he said. He gave a low, graceful bow.

Then he opened his arms. Everyone fell silent. Being careful to keep quiet, Margot shifted so she could see better. The storyteller's fingertips started glowing with the pale yellow light of magic. The light spread down his arms like vines growing fast. It wrapped around him and became an illusion. He was Rosalind. She wore a draping gown of pale red, and her brown hair hung to her knees. Her face was clever and merry. To Margot, everyone else seemed hazy and indistinct. Rosalind was real.

> "The third daughter of the strongest chieftain was
> clever fair Rosalind,
> but her father heard
> that one man would take from him his place
> as chieftain,
> would cast him down:
> the man who married Rosalind.

> "He took her to his brother,
> a trader in forbidden magics,
> who made her fair face, her fair hair
> disappear.
> In their place was the head
> of a pig."

Rosalind's face stretched. Her eyes shrank. Her hair disappeared. Her nose lengthened and fattened into a snout. She cried and raged. Margot winced. The cries were hard to listen to.

Then Rosalind left her father. The holy men could do nothing but tell her she'd have to wed to break the spell. So she looked in cities and in countrysides for a man she could marry. While her gown faded and tore, her boots wore thin and cracked. Then, in a field, on a sunny day, she met a man who stopped his hunting to talk to her. His name was Gregoire.

*"Each day, he'd say he'd not come back.*
*But then he returned*
*and lingered*
*and laughed with her,*
*until one day he had too much game to carry home.*

*"'I don't like to leave my catch behind,'*
*he said.*
*'I'll take a bundle for you if you wish,'*
*she said.*
*They walked in the hot sun*
*together,*
*until they had to stop*
*to sit and rest beside the path.*

*"And Gregoire saw*
*that her hands were very lovely,*
*as were her ankles, and the shape of her,*
*beneath her gown.*
*'Besides your pig's head,' he said,*
*'you're the fairest woman I've ever seen.'*
*'When I marry, the pig's head will disappear,'*
*she answered.*
*'The spell cast by my uncle will break,*
*and the face I had, my face, will return.'*
*'If that's so,' he said,*
*'and if you'll have me,*
*I'll rid you of that pig's head as soon as I am able.'"*

Margot felt as if moths were fluttering in her chest, wings
brushing against each other and her ribs. The spell was almost
broken. Gregoire and Rosalind went to a holy man, who per-

formed the rites and bound their wedding bands to their fingers. Then Rosalind stepped forward. The wings in Margot beat harder.

Rosalind's head, the pig's head, began to narrow and shrink. The snout and jowls became a woman's clever, merry face. The squinty eyes grew larger and almond shaped. Brown wavy hair flowed over her shoulders. Rosalind laughed. So did Margot. There were other sounds, cheering, far away. Only Rosalind's triumphant laughter ringing out with Margot's was loud and real.

Gregoire fought Rosalind's father and won. He and Rosalind ruled the land. *"And if they'd lived forever, they'd be with us still."* Rosalind curtseyed, laughing again.

Then Rosalind faded.

A man, the storyteller, stood where she'd been. Another man stepped into the space cleared around the storyteller, a tall, bearded man in a rich blue tunic, Margot's father. Margot's grin melted away. The king had an arm around Belinde, whose jeweled combs glinted in her hair. He and his queen praised the tale teller. The merchant's daughters standing beside Margot on the bench whispered. Margot could hear snatches of conversation from the cousins and the aunts and uncles. She could smell their sweat and the flower scents they used. Why couldn't they have faded instead of Rosalind?

Margot's father still had a protective arm around Belinde, but he'd most likely put her aside as quickly as he'd put aside any other woman. He might like a love story, but he'd place Margot in any advantageous match—advantageous for him. He'd even arrange a barren match, one made for alliance only, not love at all. Margot leaned against the wall behind her. People pitied women in barren matches, or laughed at them. She pressed hard against the solid, unyielding stones. If she were water, she'd run out through the cracks that let in the drafts. Then she'd be free.

⟍☉⟋

Margot left the feast earlier than almost anyone else. She went through the entrance hall's side door. Then, with defiant pleasure, she started down the steps to the holy men's stone-paved tunnels: girls were forbidden to walk dark, remote places alone. Demon spirits wanted to rule not just their realms deep under the ground but also the god's realms beyond the clouds, and human lands, too. They used their magics to burrow up from deep in the earth. They made doorways in lonely roads, alleys, and underground walkways. Then they took over abandoned houses and enslaved people and animals. But demon spirits were rarely found in the holy men's tunnels. The holy men walked through often, easily noticed any weakening spells, and fixed them. Men and even older boys walked here alone all the time. These men weren't just herbalists and storytellers, whose magics gave them a little protection from demon spirits. They were also scrubs or lords, any men. Woman minstrels, however, weren't allowed alone in the tunnels, though they had magics like those of the herbalists and storytellers. Margot had once overheard Belinde say that women could walk alone in the city she'd come from. The king and the holy men there thought it safe. Margot's father had said, teasing, that that was one of her city's flaws. Margot hadn't heard the rest of the discussion. Still, she was glad she'd heard so much. She kept a list in her head of rules that made little sense or were not the same everywhere. These rules were proof that holy men could be wrong about all kinds of things, not just about her.

She walked along the stone path. Dim lanterns lit her way. The click of her wooden boot heels echoed eerily, and she caught herself glancing sideways into the shadows. She thought of demon spirits. They were old; the demon had made them long ago, after he'd grown out of the rock, fire, and muck deep underground. Despite this, they had beautiful faces. They also had a boggy, rotting stench that she'd never seen or smelled but knew to run from. It was stupid to feel so jittery. No demon spirit had ever appeared in this tunnel. Just because she was a girl didn't mean they would do so now.

She stopped looking into the shadows and, finally, exited the passageway when she reached the small wooden tunnel shed. The libaria, the eating hall, and all the other houses that made up the holy men's draelan were quiet and dark. She tramped through the vegetable garden, wet from the rain she'd missed standing in. At the garden's end she avoided the path to the cairns, where the holy men waited for rare visits and advice from the god's spirits. She made her way to one of the squat guesthouses. The door creaked as she stepped into the one cramped room. It had a narrow bed and a simple bench and table. She had to sleep in this room for a few nights while important cousins stayed in her room. She didn't mind. A fire in the hearth already warmed it, and she suddenly felt twelve instead of fifteen. For a year, she'd lived in a house like this one; an earlier of her father's wives had thought "it would be best." The wife had wanted the holy men to spend more time teaching her to stop acting like a fortuneteller's daughter. Belinde had brought her back to the castle. The new queen wanted her nearby to find her a husband more easily. As did her father.

She stirred the coals and added wood to the fire. Then she got into the narrow bed. She reached under her pillows, defiant pleasure rising in her again. She pulled out the most precious of all her possessions: a book the length and width of one hand span. She lifted it to her nose and breathed in deeply. It should have smelled of leather and vellum, but it didn't and never had. It smelled as the Sea must smell, of water-drenched wind and inexplicable wildness. When she lowered it from her face, she could taste salt on her tongue.

With one finger, Margot traced the embossed words on the cover. The letters were shaped unlike any she'd ever seen, full of odd twists and curls. They spelled *The Book of the Sea.*

Slowly, reverently, she opened the book. On the first page, in angular cramped letters, was a name—Maira Alys of Isles of Pristanne—Margot's mother. Above this name were others—Tegwen Lassair of Isles, Ariana Elin of Isles. Margot ran her fingertip over them, as if her skin would soak up their meaning. Were they grandmothers, aunts, cousins? No family members from the Western Isles had come to her mother's funeral. None had ever written or visited. Her father refused to speak of his dead queen's family. Except for this book, it was as if her mother had come from no one and nowhere.

Margot was lucky even to have the book. When she was three and her mother had just died, she'd once been left alone near a box of leftover odds and ends. She'd seen the book lying on top as if it had been flung in. She'd taken it and pressed it against her face. Its smell had been like her mother's. Hugging it close, she had wandered back to her nursery. She remembered how she'd lain on her favorite soft blanket, curled around the book.

Its own kind of magic had kept it hidden from her various nursescrubs. When she was a child, she'd often found it put away, leaning next to the one other book on her shelf. It had looked very strange and out of place next to the small bright book that had family history verses in it. Yet no one else had seemed to notice. She had thought it her secret friend, as a child. Now she knew that only girls who apprenticed to minstrels used or touched magic, so she helped it stay hidden. The holy men would take it if they knew about it. It wasn't theirs to have.

Margot began to turn the pages. The first letter on each page was large with intricate patterns. *J*s had the shape of creatures with horses' heads and fishes' bodies. *W*s looked like water pushed and pulled in a storm. Letters sat together, each one arching unfamiliarly but still full of meaning: whirlpool, reef, current, tide. No words or pictures had anything to do with fortunetelling or love potions, thievery or trickery. They told of Sea animals and plants. They described how the seasons changed the water. They explained what lived in the shallow and deep pools. Margot bent over the book, her cheek against her hand. The pull of the words caught her up and carried her away.

The flame flickered. Startled, Margot looked up. The candle had burned down to a nub. She closed the book and rubbed her aching eyes. The light would be gone soon, but she flipped to the book's last several pages, where the writing changed. The letters were angular and pushed close together. This was her mother's writing.

Margot read of the waters her mother had found around this castle and land, Pristanne. She seemed to have loved Pristanne's small, merry rivers and the wide, placid lake outside the castle gardens. Then Margot wrapped her arms tightly around herself and read:

> I need to go home to the Sea. The air isn't the same here. It's so dull and dry. My lungs only half fill, and then I hack and choke. I need to sit and breathe air that's thick with water. Philip, I think, finally understands that I have to go, and that I'll come back.

*I'll take little Margot. She'll love the Sea. I know*
*she will. We'll leave soon, when spring comes.*

Margot closed the book and tucked it under her pillow. Her mother hadn't reached the Sea again. She'd died that spring of a sickness in her lungs. Margot had been so close to going to a place where no one would scorn her.

She pulled up her knees and rested her forehead on them. Her mother was gone, but out beyond the mountains were the lands near the Sea, the westlands. Beyond them were the Western Isles and her mother's family, or at least people like her. Both were a long, dangerous journey away. To travel to them, she needed gold she didn't have to pay a holy man to protect her from demon spirits. Even if she had the gold, she didn't know any holy man who would help her run away. Traveling alone would be difficult, impossible.

Animal sounds a long way off made her look to the small window and its barred shutter. Outside, many feral voices shrieked and ululated. It was probably just a pack of wild dogs. It could be demon spirits, though, triumphing over a capture or sounding a challenge.

If they were calling a challenge, it wasn't for her. But the cries seemed to be taunting her. *You're too scared. You won't run.*

They were wrong. Margot went to the window, unbarred the shutter, and opened it a crack. She stared at the night-shrouded path. She couldn't see any creatures, spirit or otherwise, but she felt she was staring something down. She'd run. Soon.

he next midmorning, Margot walked through the
freshly scrubbed feast room. Except for her, it was
empty. She was often able to roam alone, as long
as she stayed quiet and off to the side. Other people went about their tasks. She went about hers: trying to think
of some way to escape.

She caught a glimpse of cousins on the stairs. They wore
their second-best gowns and were adjusting each other's hair.
Isabeau was in the center, directing the rest. Today was a market day. They were going to the lace and silk stalls. Which was
fine with Margot; she wouldn't have to work hard to avoid
them.

Before they noticed her, Margot slipped into the entrance
hall, then into the dim side hallway. The cousins passed
through the entrance hall, as raucous as jaybirds. She stayed
where she was. There were only two doors in this hallway, one
to the queen's sitting room and one to her father's. Listening
in wasn't honorable. But it was how she learned what everyone
else, from the queen to the stableboys, knew. When her father
had decided to put his last two wives aside, no one had told her.
She'd found out here. She'd also found out, just recently, that

the holy men thought she should marry soon. And when she was lucky, she heard about the westlanders. She liked hearing about them, though much of what was said was said nastily. They lived close to the Sea; they were supposed to be more like those from the Western Isles. One of their kings came over the mountains each year with swordsmen, laborers, and great casks of wine. He traded wine for as many tall, thick trees as he could get. The westlanders had cut most of theirs down, except for the sickly ones. They needed the wood for building big boats. Margot had thought many times of trying to run to the trading westlanders. Anyone who had boats that rode the Sea must understand more about water than people here. She didn't know if they'd help her, however, even if she could find a way to get to them. They might return her to her father. Still, she listened in and wondered.

She went down the hallway and stopped by the door to the queen's sitting room. As always, she felt suddenly more awake and watchful. Giving a quick glance over her shoulder, she crouched, as if adjusting her boot. She shifted a little closer to the warped section of the door, where it no longer met the frame well. She heard laughter and talk about stitching. She stared at the floor rushes, which were old but still sweet smelling. More laughter, more talk of stitching. She tapped the toe of her boot with her fingers. This wasn't so interesting.

The chattering changed; the women speculated about which storyteller might visit this summer. Restless, Margot stood.

Now she couldn't stop thinking that many people traveled in the summer, from storytellers to kings. People were moving, going. She wasn't.

She turned and headed back toward the entrance hall.

Ahead, around the corner, came Holy Charles, her father's favorite holy man advisor. Concern and a kind of elation went through her; she was good at not getting caught. She didn't hunch with guilt. She kept walking quietly. If she looked as if she were supposed to be here, people believed she was. Few ever stopped or accused her.

Holy Charles gave her a bow. He was shorter than she was, but something about him always made her feel small. Maybe the way his eyes gave her a quick, dissatisfied up-and-down look. He went by. She allowed herself a little smile.

Then, from behind her, she heard a door open. The holy man said, "Highness."

"Holy Charles," came Belinde's voice. Margot's smile disappeared. She wasn't entirely free yet. "Would you please tell the king I'll be there in a moment."

"Of course, Highness."

If Belinde had meant to see the king, why had she said "in a moment"? Not because the queen had seen her, Margot hoped. She tried not to quicken her pace. Hurrying would make her seem as if she was running from something.

"Princess," called the queen. Reluctantly, Margot stopped.

"Yes, Highness?" she asked. She didn't know what Belinde would do about her listening in, if Belinde realized. She turned, back straight, giving nothing away.

The queen's hair, as always, was perfectly braided and pinned. Although she'd been stitching, her gown hung over her belly and down without any extra wrinkles or stray threads. "Could you join me?" she asked, pronouncing every word distinctly, as, she'd once explained, all city people did.

"Yes, Highness," Margot repeated, wishing she could say no.

Belinde leaned into the room and said something. A

horse-faced aunt, Aunt Cinda, came briskly out and walked down the hallway. She didn't bother to say good morning. Margot followed the queen into the room. The window shutters were open, letting in sunlight. The air smelled faintly of lavender. A woven white cloth was stretched on a large frame. Red and blue stitches danced across it. The stitches made birds, Margot saw. She stopped by one of the high-backed chairs. Belinde closed the door, then came over. Her eyes were serious and her lips were pursed. Feeling grim, Margot thought she was caught for sure, but only waited.

"You didn't go with the others to town?" Belinde asked.

"Not today," Margot answered. She was suddenly very aware that her gown was dirty from crouching on the floor. "They've left already?" she asked, hoping to fix the queen's attention on the cousins instead of her gown.

"I expect so. You should have gone with them." Belinde didn't say this the way the other wives would have, as if they wanted to see her as little as possible and hated every chance she missed to be far away from them. The queen spoke with exasperation. "You should always go. You should smile and talk like the others."

Margot replied, "I suppose so," wary of what might come next.

"That's not much of an answer," Belinde said. She sat in the chair and rested her hands in her lap. "You're stubborn, but you go about things the wrong way. A woman can get what she wants, always." Belinde's tone had changed. She sounded as if she were saying aloud things she wouldn't say to just anyone. She sounded as if she were telling a secret. Not to Isabeau or the aunts, to Margot. "It's harder here than it is in my city. That's for certain. In my city, women travel alone even in the holy men's tunnels. They have feasts for discussing magics.

The holy men don't think these things against the god's rules. But there are still men who believe women should obey and be silent, like many men here. You really can't cringe or snap every time they—or even other women—stand in your way. You make them feel clever, you choose your moment to speak, you win them over.

"To be plain," Belinde went on, her tone still confiding, "if you wanted the crown, I wouldn't like you so much. I'm queen here, and plan to be the mother of a king or queen. You don't want to stay, though. Others might not notice, but I think it easy to see. You hope to go west, or run off to live with fortunetellers." The queen frowned with distaste. "Whatever you've been dreaming about." Then the frown lifted, and she continued, "Regardless, you want more than to be always taunted. You'll fight to have what you want. I honor you for that. I can help you."

Margot didn't know what to say. She tried to gather her thoughts, half hating Belinde for not understanding about water, half loving her for saying "honor": *I honor you.* "What do you mean, help?"

"Troupes of fortunetellers travel around. I could tell you when they're near. Or there are the westlanders. They've come farther east this year. A few lords have invited them in, because of one of their holy men. His people call him Demon Spirits' Bane," said Belinde thoughtfully. "I've heard it said he can call up a wind. Like the kind used for rites, but stronger. He's able to fight demon spirits' noxious winds and blinding lights. I've also heard it said demon spirits don't walk his lands anymore, or carry off his people to drudge underground. Your father could be convinced to speak with him.

"My help may not get you what you've been hoping for, but it could. Depending on what you make of it." Belinde waited, looking Margot more squarely in the face than people usually did.

Margot knew the queen wanted her gone because of the baby and the crown. But she was offering help for the kind of escape Margot wanted.

Belinde wasn't just planning to force her into a barren marriage. "I've wanted—" Margot's voice was croaky. She cleared her throat. The westlanders might think she should come with them, or they might think she belonged here. She wouldn't know what they thought if she didn't meet them. "I've wondered about the westlanders."

Belinde nodded once in her delicate, precise way. "I'll see what I can do." Then she looked pointedly at Margot's gown. "I also have to tell you that I won't crouch outside your door if you'll stop crouching outside mine."

Belinde smiled, but Margot had the feeling that if she didn't agree to this, the queen might actually listen in on her. "I'll stop," Margot said.

"Very good," said Belinde. "Don't waste the day," she added, which was what the cousins always called as they left each other.

"Nor you." Margot's response came easily, though she'd never said it before. She walked out of the room slowly, the conversation rushing through her mind again and again.

∽⟨ତ⟩∾

For days and days, Margot kept going over everything Belinde had said to her. She wondered about the city where women had more freedom. Mostly, however, she wondered what Belinde was saying to her father and whether she'd succeed in bringing the westlanders here. What the westlanders might then do, Margot wasn't sure; she imagined wildly good possibilities, wildly awful ones, and everything in between.

But after a while, Margot almost thought she'd imagined her conversation with her stepmother. Everything was as it always had been. Belinde spent her time in the sitting room or the garden. She didn't ask to see Margot. People mentioned the westlanders, often speaking of the holy man called Demon Spirits' Bane and the magic he was supposed to have. Then they'd fall silent, as if struck dumb by the possibility that a westlander might know something their holy men didn't. After that, they'd dismiss the rumor as ridiculous gossip. No one said the westlanders were coming. At times, when Margot was sure she hadn't imagined the talk, she suspected that Belinde had been teasing her and was laughing behind her back. She started avoiding the queen. She hadn't hated her before. Now she did.

Margot couldn't bear the castle or anyone in it. She walked through its main entrance, crossed the courtyard, and left by its outer gate. She ignored the swordsmen on guard. They kept talking, ignoring her. She went a few steps along the dirt road, then stopped and looked down the hill.

Below, in the valley, was the great town with all its crowded buildings and winding paths. Beyond was the wall that encircled the town, the castle, and the small lake. It was twelve feet high and made of stone, with invisible spells in the mortar to keep demon spirits out. Holy men walked on it. They sought spells broken by weather, or by criminals who wanted to earn demon spirits' rewards: potent poisons, cruelly charmed weapons, sometimes even dangerous spells that flashed and blinded. Swordsmen were on watch for criminals, as well; they also walked the wall and manned the great log gate. To run away, she would have to get over the high stone wall or through the wood gate. She shaded her eyes from the sun with one hand. As if that would help. The gate was still there. So were the wall, the swordsmen, and the holy men. Over or through, through or over. She had to think.

The wall was the first difficulty, but not the only one. She looked beyond it, at the curving brown road. The strip of brown led from the gate, swerved around a forest, and joined a larger road. Green fields and forests lay all around the larger road. Along it, and the others that split from it, stood a few narrow, jutting castles. They, too, had walls that surrounded their fields and draelans, houses and shacks. Some who went out of the walls paid holy men silver to travel with them and protect them. Others traveled as storytellers and minstrels did in the summers—they took the risk that they'd find a lord's castle or a village before each night fell. Unlike storytellers, Margot had nothing to trade for lodging. She was no nearer an answer than she'd been before. Her thoughts went in a circle: the wall, the gate, no coin. The circle seemed complete, unbreakable.

She turned and walked quickly. She passed the castle and veered around its corner. She went on through the flower garden and its blooming summer lilies, past the fenced vegetable and herb gardens. Now she could see the willows and the small lake, a stretch of brown-green most just called the washing water. She ran down the hill, which was bare of buildings on this side because the lake was so near. The water's surface rippled here and there as the wind brushed against it. Mostly, though, it was calm and satin smooth. She hiked up her skirt and ran faster.

She reached the lake, stopped, and squatted. She wanted to tug off her boots and walk in until the water was all around her. It would seep through her thin undergown. It would touch her belly and back. She looked down at her reflection, at her too-pale, too-angular face. Then she looked deeper into the water that always, no matter how troubled or upset she was, made her feel better.

She could really think if she was lying in the lake, face to the sky. But night was the only time she could secretly swim. She'd done it a few times each summer, risking capture by swordsmen, holy men, or demon spirits someone had helped through the wall. Her book said fish and other Sea creatures glided and floated, so she'd taught herself to do the same. No one else here could or would. They thought swimming was only for frogs and other muddy animals. Many also thought it was fortunetelling magic, like making weak love potions. A blade of grass floated near her. Envious, she lowered her face to it and breathed in the scent of cool fresh water, the previous night's rain. There was a way out. If she could lie as the grass did, surrounded, held up, she could find it.

The lake lapped at her boots and muddy skirt hem. She dipped her fingers into the coolness. Ahead and above, the swordsmen stood in their scattered places on the wall. They were on watch for criminals, but were watching her, too. She stirred the water, and it glided around her fingers the way it would glide over her arms and legs. She wasn't going to swim in front of the swordsmen, but she'd never been so tempted while they were watching.

Then her attention snagged on something, someone, else. A man walked from the willows at the far side of the water. She stared; no one walked among those trees except her.

He made his way around the lake. As he came nearer, she saw he was dressed in a brown overtunic. It was embroidered with three signs, one for the god's sky realms, one for the demon's underground realms, and one for the humans' land realms: he was a holy man who, because he wore brown instead of gray or red, didn't live in a draelan. Those were rare. Rarer still was a holy man who wore silver circlets on his brow and around his wrists, which meant he was a noble of some kind, and ruled land. He was also very tall. His hair was a rare color, light yellow. Margot stood, glancing at the trees he'd been in, then back at him. He came straight toward her, almost as if he'd been searching for her. He stopped, inclined his head, and smiled. "King Orrin of Mawr. I arrived late last night, unexpectedly," he said. His speech had an almost singing rhythm. "I think you must be the princess?"

She understood now. He was the kind who liked grotesque attractions. She met many who wanted to see every three-headed calf, every tree knot that looked like a chicken, and her. "Princess Margot of Pristanne, Highness," she answered bluntly, ready to go once he made his nasty response.

Instead, his smile grew broader. "I was hoping you were. I've been traveling through the midlands since early summer, for trade and talks about fighting demon spirits," he said in his foreign-sounding rhythm. "I have to admit I heard of you as we were traveling. Your stepmother also mentioned you, when we arrived. I've been wanting to meet you. Your mother was from the Western Isles, wasn't she? Mawr is in the westlands, by the Sea. Have you ever made the hard trip to the Isles? They're beautiful, I've heard."

Margot could see the light wind ripple the lake but couldn't feel it. This was the westlander holy man she and Belinde had spoken of. He lived on the Sea. He spoke of the Western Isles as beautiful. Belinde had wanted him to come, and had made sure he had. "No, Highness," she heard herself say.

"Yet you must have visited the West. What do you think of the Sea?" he asked with an intent stare.

That stare was too much like the ones the holy men here gave her; they peered at her all the time while they asked questions, and none of her answers was ever right. She kept thoughts about the Sea to herself and answered, warily, "I haven't seen it."

The smile left his face, making his hooked nose seem more bent and his chin more pointed. "You don't need to sound so suspicious. It's a magnificent, powerful thing. And its ways and secrets have nothing to do with base fortunetelling magic," he responded, his words clipped.

He'd said, out loud, what she'd thought alone, inside, for so long. A light sparked in Margot. "I know," she answered quickly. "I didn't mean to offend you. I just have to be careful what I say here."

"Of course. I'm sorry. I should have realized," he said, his face softening. Margot just nodded; she'd never had an apology from a holy man before. "Midlanders," he went on, "are so ignorant about water and the Sea. They don't even know it, that's what angers me. And my midlander brethren are as ignorant as the rest. Have they given you bad headaches trying to make some spell to drain the 'tainted blood' out of you? Do they lecture nonsense about the Sea at you whenever they can?" He smiled again, but his smile seemed sad. "They're supposed to speak truth, and instead they are sometimes no better than the heathens who live in the ice lands."

He knew. He understood. "They used to. Now they avoid me, as long as I'm quiet," Margot answered, the light inside her blazing stronger. "Are you the holy man they call Demon Spirits' Bane? Can you tell me about the westlands? About the Sea? Everything?"

"I didn't know that name had traveled this far. Yes, I am." He grinned but glanced at the sky, saying, "I have to meet with your father and the others. I don't want to insult them by being late. You'll be at tonight's feast?" She nodded again, and he said, "I'll look forward to talking with you then." He held out his hand.

Margot looked at the hand for a moment, at the rings on

each of his fingers and the smooth underside of his wrist, before realizing he wanted hers to kiss. People never kissed her hand. With him, she was normal and everyone here was backward.

She reached out. His hand was cool. He bent and his lips brushed her skin. Goose flesh rose on her arms. She felt not just lit up but flushed.

She watched him start toward the castle with a long, purposeful stride. She liked his kiss a little too much. Yet she didn't care if he courted her, not really. She didn't care if he said she was pretty or not, only that he was here and would tell her about the westlands. His coming had proved there was a place for her, a home. She had to escape and get to it. He might even help her.

"The king wants to see you, Princess," said a young voice, startling Margot. She hadn't noticed that a scrawny boy, Tiss, the cook's youngest, had come down the hillside. He pointed toward the castle. Then he glanced at his feet to make sure he hadn't somehow stepped too close to the lake without noticing. "He says hurry up because he has other things to do. I'm supposed to walk you in."

If her father had seen her by the lake, he'd be angry. Margot grinned, thinking of what King Orrin had called midlanders: *ignorant.* "I can get there myself. I know the way."

The boy wrinkled his nose. He probably wanted to hear the king go on at her. She ran up the hillside ahead of him, guessing rightly that he wouldn't run and risk looking silly trying to catch her. She raced through the gardens. Then she stopped before going into the castle and caught her breath. In the last year or so, she'd found that it was easier to be silent and dull with her father. When she didn't make a sound, didn't fight, didn't push to make him feel as bad as he made her feel, he said less to her. Not that she always succeeded in keeping quiet.

As she walked in the door, she realized that she wasn't succeeding in keeping quiet now. She couldn't stop thinking of how Belinde had said she'd help and then had done so. Margot wanted to talk with her alone. She'd like to thank her and maybe hear her say, "I honor you" again. She also couldn't stop thinking of King Orrin, and of every word he'd said. Finally, finally, things might be changing for her. And so it was hard to walk softly; her boots thudded. She slowed as she crossed the entrance hall. She stepped with more care. That was better. She'd be silent, barely noticeable. She'd go in, he'd say what he wanted, she'd leave.

He sat in one of the high-backed oak chairs. He had black hair and a black beard. His eyes were black, and he had olive skin. No one had ever accused him of looking like anything other than a midlander. "Close the door," he instructed, his voice calm until she had obeyed him. Then he said, "Well? What were you doing by the lake? You were alone with a westlander. Half the front of your gown is wet and covered in mud. What were you thinking?"

*Ignorant*, Margot silently insulted him, but her earlier lit-up happiness suddenly seemed far, far away. He was wrong but thought he was right. "Nothing," she said, staying dull.

"Nothing isn't an answer." His words shoved at her.

She wanted to shove back with the truth. Her shoulders were stiff. They could barely shrug her answer.

"It was stupid," he said. "It was wrong."

"It wasn't," she retorted, unable to tolerate *his* calling *her* wrong. "King Orrin is a holy man. He was at the lake, too."

"He may be a holy man, but he's a westlander. People expect that of him, and won't care much as long as he brings good trade, tells us what he's learned of magic and demon spirits, then leaves. You're a midlander who needs a husband. You can see the difference. You're not dim," he answered, standing. "Every one of your cousins would have known better than to stand there talking with him, alone, if they met accidentally. I can't believe you didn't realize that the less you see of the westlanders, the better. As to the lake, I'll admit it's my fault you have base blood. But you make things far worse for yourself when you refuse to avoid water. How do you expect me to find you a husband?"

"I don't. I shouldn't even be here. You've been to the westlands, you know that's where I belong," she said, her voice raw in her throat. He wouldn't understand. She had to say it anyway, before she left here forever. "You should have sent me to the Western Isles and the Sea. My mother wanted me to go. She wanted to take me."

Her father's face went gray. He'd never hit her before, or anyone else, outside the competition ring or battlefield, but she crossed her arms, sure he was going to now. Then she realized his black eyes weren't angry. They were filled with a sorrow that seemed bottomless. She had seen him look this way long ago but had forgotten. It had been when she was very young and had asked him about her mother.

He still loved her mother. He called his first wife tainted and their marriage a mistake, but he still loved her. He could have told Margot this, just once. Her fingers interlaced and gripped each other. If this love meant that he'd send her west to the Sea because of her mother's wishes, she wouldn't care anymore what he did or didn't do.

He finally said, each word quiet but clear, "I have no heir, yet, and your husband might someday rule here. My marrying a westlander woman was one thing. Marrying you to a westlander, possibly making a westlander king here, would cause rebellion or war. My selfishness has made enough difficulty; I won't have yours tear our family's lands to pieces. I'm certainly not sending you off unmarried, for no purpose at all. Now leave me."

Margot stepped back as he turned away, dismissing her. Then she walked swiftly from the room, slamming the door behind her. She'd go, and she'd never talk to him again.

# Three

fter returning to her guesthouse, Margot realized she couldn't talk to King Orrin at the feast. Too many people would notice and whisper. But her father had forgotten that with the cousins in her room, she was staying in the draelan, and that the westlanders were also staying here. So, thanks to the small window, she could make sure she "accidentally" met him as he walked near. She watched for him. She went over and over what she might ask him about the Sea and what he might say back. When she saw him and the other westlander holy man, the one with the long mustache, make their way toward their guesthouse, she stepped out her door.

Once outside, Margot went to the edge of the broad, flat step. They hadn't seen her yet. Should she call out? Now she didn't know what to ask. Not one thing she'd thought of saying earlier seemed graceful or clever.

He saw her, raised a hand, and started to walk over. He was a head taller than almost everyone else she knew, and brighter, too, with his yellow hair hanging around his shoulders. She smiled. He smiled. That wasn't a bad start.

He stopped near the turn to her door. "We were just going

back to our house. This is Holy Meynard." The other holy man bowed; Margot curtseyed. "I'll be there in a moment," said King Orrin. Holy Meynard nodded, then went on.

"I hear from your father that you aren't supposed to talk much with westlanders," King Orrin remarked, his smile fading. "People here would whisper, because they don't think much of us."

Margot's smile fell. Maybe he'd only come over to say he couldn't talk to her. "I know, but I wanted to hear more about the Sea," she said. She had to slow down, she was speaking too fast.

King Orrin studied his hands. "I'm your father's guest. You owe him obedience. I need his trade now, and I'll need midlander trade in the future." He was silent. Margot's mind raced, trying to think of some way to convince him. "But I hate to be ruled by ignorance," he went on. "Holy men do sometimes disobey kings, when it's for the best. That you don't know much about the Sea isn't fair or right."

"It isn't," Margot answered. She willed him to decide to go against her father.

"As I said, I hate to be ruled by ignorance." He looked up, his smile back. "I think we can talk a little."

"I'd like that," Margot said. She'd never been so happy. "If I mention water at all, they call me a fortuneteller."

"A fortuneteller. They haven't named me that to my face, but one of your father's holy men was lecturing me earlier about how my people have a weakness for base magics. He offered to come teach in my land." King Orrin gave a barking laugh that at first was sharp but then became pleased. "Him teach us. The midlands have enough problems for him and his brethren, I hear, with the demon spirits."

"They really aren't as bad in the West?" Margot asked. She'd be glad if the holy men here were made to admit that a west-lander had done something they themselves hadn't.

"I don't mean to say we've destroyed the demon spirits. We certainly haven't fought or attacked them underground. We don't even have anyone who's gone down to the slime and fire and returned, as great heroes of the oldest age did. But we might one day, and maybe then we'll think of how to crush or burn their passageways and cities." He sounded determined.

"For now, Mawr simply has fewer demon spirits than other places," he went on. "I've found a way to stop them from in-festing our land, or at least a way to hinder them more. I've trained holy men to hunt them down. I have stricter rules to stop criminals who'd trade for forbidden magics." He shook his head. "Ever summer, a different westlander king leads the trade journey. I came this summer because I meant to talk of our success in driving out demon spirits, as well as trade wine for wood. I thought midlanders would finally have to admit they shouldn't think us base. All the lands could be safer, and we could build stronger alliances, trade more. Kings and lords here have been eager to hear what I have to say. Even those who don't have trees to spare offered feasts and asked for advice. The midlanders don't really think better about us, though. My men and I still can't speak of the Sea, not in sitting rooms or at feasts, not by a fire, after food," he said.

Margot envied the longing for the Sea she heard in his voice. "What's worst about being away from it?"

"I miss the smell. It's always thick, wet, and salty. Some-times it's rotten, like fish lying out on the docks; and some-times it's wild, blowing hard; or fresh, a cold, early-morning smell. I also miss seeing water stretching on all around." He spoke to her eagerly. "I miss its depths. It hides things under-neath, secrets. Fishermen or boatmen spend their whole lives trying to learn even a few of them, like how different currents move or where vast schools of fish hide. And the Sea hides other secrets, as well." He frowned.

"Like what?" Margot asked. The rest of the draelan, the castle, everything seemed very far from this small haven outside her door. "Do you know them?"

His frown lifted. "They wouldn't be secrets then, would they? No. Fishermen and boatmen claim to have seen creatures now and then. They've said there are glowing horses in the waves, or monstrous serpents. Lights."

She couldn't tell if he was teasing her. "Really?"

"The Sea's amazing. Like nothing else." He told her about a boat lost in a storm and washed up months later, whole but empty. He also said a boatman had once sailed with a huge serpent's skull on his ship's prow. The boatman had claimed he'd fought and beaten the serpent near one of the Western Isles. "I've been out in a wind that was like pure fury," King Orrin went on. "It came off the Sea. I was scared it would pick me up and carry me away. This was just two years ago. I was eighteen, not a boy, but I really thought it might. I crouched behind a boulder, holding on to crevices. I'd never felt anything like it before. No one had, not even the oldest holy man in the draelan." Margot nodded. She didn't want to be on this doorstep. She wanted to touch that abandoned ship and the serpent's skull, to be in that wind.

"Then there are people like you." King Orrin again had the intent, holy man stare that immediately set Margot on her guard. She made herself loosen her arms and hands; he wasn't like the rest. "People with raven hair and cream skin," he went on. "You don't seem to have webs between your fingers, but I've heard you know things about water no one's ever told you. You have water in your blood, don't you?"

It sounded too much as though he was asking, in another way, if she had tainted blood, except that his tone wasn't sharp or unkind. "I don't know what you mean," she said.

"I forgot. Of course. It's not a bad thing," he explained, as if noticing her unease. "A few people know water better than others. They even know some of its secrets, like animals that fishermen have only glimpsed. Or currents that rarely appear. They haven't seen these things; they just know about them. In my land, you'd be consulted by fine boat builders, boatmen, and anyone who travels over the water or uses it. They'd ask your advice."

He seemed very sure he was right, but she wasn't. "This knowing comes from blood, not learning or reading? Like from a book?" she asked.

"It's in the blood, much more in the blood than other magical talents. If a child's family wants him to be a holy man, they'll take him to a draelan. Holy men there will touch his hands. If they feel a mild power in the boy, and if one of them chooses him, he'll become an apprentice to learn more of our craft. Then he'll inherit the master's full power before the master dies. He's chosen, he learns, he inherits.

"Those with water in their blood are simply born with the full gift or not. It's very rare. No one knows where it comes from. Some holy men say it's from women, long ago, who craved and drank Sea water before they gave birth. Others say some people were fish before, and that these people have passed their blood down. A few claim the gift comes from seal women who married men. These seals are said to be more animal than person, though. And I know of no man who's seen or caught one, let alone mated with one."

His stare was still fixed on her, and it made her muscles wind tighter again. The names in her book simply seemed women's names, not those of seal women or fish women or women who thirsted for the Sea. She didn't inexplicably know about water, either; she'd learned what she knew from her reading. "I've never heard of those kinds of women," she said carefully. He talked of the Sea so easily; it was hard to avoid mentioning her book. "I understand some about the water, but not lots."

"No one's taught you what you do know. That's certain," he said.

She surely wasn't going to claim she'd learned about water from someone *here.* "They haven't. I can't even mention water," she answered.

He looked away, not staring or prying no matter how she responded, the way her father's advisors often had. "I'm sorry," he said. "But if that's so, then you might have water in your blood. Think on it."

Letting the topic lie, he began telling her about the rocks and caves in the cliffs on Mawr's shoreline. He said there once was a very dim band of fishermen who got lost in the caves and kept wandering around in circles. He meant, she thought, to make her smile. And as he described the way they feared their own voices' echoes, she did. She couldn't tell him how she knew about water, but she could talk to him about a lot. She loved listening to him, too.

The next day, Belinde called Margot into her sitting room. "If you've met with the westlanders, you've been good about doing it where no one can see," Belinde said approvingly. Margot beamed. She and King Orrin hadn't spoken at the feast. She'd liked how they'd walked by each other and stood in different parts of the hall, so everyone thought they'd never talked.

"It was hard to convince your father to bring them," Belinde went on. "In the end we had to invite them without seeming to invite them. I wasn't sure I could make them welcome while ensuring your father didn't think he looked like a fool. But I did it." The queen smiled in a way Margot hadn't seen before, with her teeth showing. She liked scheming, Margot realized. She liked, when much stood in her way, to get what she wanted. Margot couldn't rely on her. But because of Belinde, because of seeing that smile with the teeth showing, Margot felt she could have anything she wanted, too.

"You'll tell me what comes of this?" asked Belinde. She seemed to honestly want to find out.

"I will," said Margot, but she didn't know what there would be to tell. She hadn't confessed to King Orrin that she meant to run away. He was a westlander, but he was also a holy man, and she didn't think he'd approve.

"Good," said the queen, showing all her teeth again. Margot left her, not sure what would happen, but also smiling.

Over the next few days, she and King Orrin kept talking. She'd see him coming down the path and would step out of the guesthouse. She suspected he came down the path at about the same time every day on purpose. They stood there like any acquaintances who met in the road and had a few words. She felt like a schemer. He simply seemed to feel that these short meetings each day were the right thing to do. With this arrangement, he was doing what he thought best without going too much against her father.

Margot asked many questions, except about westlander women and magic. If women weren't allowed to know much about magic, King Orrin would wonder at her interest. Then he might ask her questions that she didn't want to answer. So she mostly asked about his land, Mawr. He told her of the capital city, Syllig. It had docks and crooked stone buildings, and cliffs on a rocky shoreline. He also told her about the vine-yards and kinds of grapes whose names she couldn't keep straight. He described traveling the roads over the mountains and into the midlands. She paid close attention, repeating what he'd told her before she went to sleep each night. She wasn't sure whether he deliberately explained the roads he'd taken because he suspected she meant to run away. He might have. But he didn't say, and so she didn't ask.

A misty drizzle fell on the fourth day. They met outside her door anyway. King Orrin seemed annoyed. His head was half bent, his answers short yeses and nos. Maybe he thought, as she'd begun to, that if anyone saw them, there might be whis-pers that they were courting. He was a holy man who was more in the world, who could marry. She studied the wet hem of her gown and her wet boot toes. Maybe he didn't like that these meetings could be mistaken for courting. A grating itch of a voice told her he might not mind, or he might have kissed her if she were someone else. She ignored the voice, which was easy since it almost sounded like Isabeau's.

She couldn't ignore his annoyance, however. He surveyed the grassy stretch between the draelan and the castle, and he didn't say anything. It could be that other problems had an-gered him. "It's wet out here," she said. She wished she could ask what was wrong, and she wished he'd tell her. As he would if she were one of his people, his friends.

"They'll keep you in the midlands," King Orrin responded abruptly.

Margot glanced at her boots, then back at him. The worry lines on his forehead and around his mouth were because of her. He was troubled over what might happen to her. "My fa-ther will try," Margot said, relishing the flash of distaste on his face. "I want to go to the westlands, or the Western Isles."

"It's just blind and backward. Whatever alliance your father makes, even if he binds your family lands to the richest in the midlands, the alliance will be a waste. It'll be like condemning a child with the talent to be a holy man to plow fields." He looked at his hands and their two sets of matching rings. "I know you're not sure you have water in your blood, but I'm sure you do. My boat builders and boatmen could use your advice about water. And we, the westlander holy men, have been trying to learn more of the Sea's secrets. You could put yourself under my draelan's protection, as an orphan or an abandoned wife would. Then you could live in the draelan by my castle. It's on the Sea. You could stay there as long as you wanted."

Margot felt as if he'd thrown open a door. She wanted to run out. But she probably didn't have water in her blood. Unless those with water in the blood weren't truly born with Sea knowledge; they had books that told of the Sea, which they kept secret, as she did. Once in the westlands, she could learn more about this. All the same, there was still the problem of getting away. "My father won't let me put myself under your protection. He won't let me leave with you."

His expression grew hard again. "I know that. I've never advised anyone to go against their father, their king, or their holy men. Yet I can't imagine condemning you to stay with all this ignorance. No one who loves water could live here. We need to find a way to free you."

That "we" wasn't a kiss or a proposal, but it pulled her close. She loved the warm nearness. "I've been trying to find a way to leave. It's difficult," she said.

"Not impossible," he said.

They stood, mostly silent, thinking of no good solution. King Orrin's men were still cutting and carrying west the wood he'd traded for. She and he needed a way to go without jeopardizing the trades he'd made, or the ones westlanders would have to make in coming summers. The grating voice inside Margot whispered that King Orrin would be courting her, would marry her to bring her west, if only she were beautiful or clever. She ignored it. She also ignored the voice nagging that talking with him might be useless: she might have to run away without help. Instead, she planned with him as if she were certain they'd leave together.

Before they came up with any answers, it was time for him to return to the castle. She stayed out, walking and thinking. She strode to the castle, then took a muddy path through the flower and herb gardens. The leaves and blossoms gave her no new ideas or reassurance. As the clouds drew back and made room for the sun, she walked the length of the largest vegetable garden. Then she slowed. Old Ildrie was talking beyond the tall, staked bean vines. Margot could see glimpses between the leaves of the old woman hanging wash, red feast cloths. Another scrub, a young, very beautiful woman named Lilla, was with her. They didn't notice Margot on the other side of bean vines. She stood still, the newly emerged sun warming her damp shoulders and head. She hadn't overheard anything important in days, only news about the litter of puppies born a few nights before and about a betrothal between two cousins who were always sneaking into dark corners together. The sun, the rustling bean leaves, and the gossiping voices seemed about to tell her something important. Maybe they'd tell her how "we," she and King Orrin, would find a way for her to put herself under his protection.

Ildrie and Lilla talked of a wedding. They had liked the bride's bright dress. They'd enjoyed the holy men's rites, which had made a wind rise and carry the binding wedding vows to the god's sky realms. Then the two women spoke of the westlanders. In a shocked whisper, Lilla said the guests wanted the tub filled when they bathed. They didn't want to stand and wash, they wanted to sit and be covered by water. "And what if *she* married one?" Lilla asked. Margot knew Lilla meant her and also knew she'd hate the answer but inched closer to the vines.

"He won't let her marry a westlander." Old Ildrie's voice wobbled with scorn. "And I heard the westlander king say he means to adopt an heir rather than marry, anyway. That's what holy men kings do, I think.

"He's a westlander," she added with disapproval, "but our king could learn something from him. If you choose an heir, then you don't get an unfit one as king. Or as queen."

Ildrie's words didn't sting as they might have at another time. Instead, Margot was filled with a surprising mixture of disappointment and triumph. She had hoped, some, that King Orrin would court her. He wouldn't. But that grating, now-silent, Isabeau-like voice had been mistaken: he didn't think her lacking. He simply wanted to stay unwed, like most holy men.

"Ildrie," Lilla was scolding. Through the leaves, Margot could see her roughly shaking out the wet feast cloths. "No westlander is better than our king."

"I'm not saying that. I'm just saying our king has that other little girl and will have the baby soon," the old woman responded. "Even if the new one's a girl, he should name one of them heir for now, in case there's no son. He says Princess Margot is base, but he likes her too much, otherwise why not put her aside and send her off somewhere?"

Lilla agreed, then began talking of a new merchant in the town. Margot picked at a bean leaf, feeling as odd as she had when she'd realized that her father continued to love her mother. Ildrie might be right about how her father felt. He certainly had secret cares no one knew existed. In the end, though, he'd still put her in a barren marriage. He'd keep her in the midlands, tied to people and a place that didn't want her. She'd escape no matter what his secret cares might be.

They talked on but said nothing helpful. Margot returned to the guesthouse. She unshuttered the small square window, glanced out at the empty path, then flopped on her mattress. She pulled her book from under her pillow. She held the book to her chest. Her thumb rubbed against the worn green leather. She bent her head and breathed in its salty scent. Holding it soothed her, made her more certain. She'd figure out how to get away.

She sat that way for a while, eyes closed, until a knock made her rush to hide the book again. Lilla, the kitchen scrub, came in to lay her fire. Margot hadn't realized how late it was. She pulled on finer stockings and her green feasting gown. Lilla helped her, a little resentfully, with laces, and then left. After rebraiding and repinning her hair, Margot left the house, too. She was surprised to find King Orrin waiting outside, in the dusk. "I'm so glad to see you," she said, pleased he'd clearly come to find her.

He gave her a quick smile. "I needed to talk to you right away," he said quietly. He drew her around the corner of the house, away from the path. He opened his mouth, closed it, then started again. "I don't know how to tell you this."

The darkness, his closeness, and the whispering all made danger seem nearby. She was worried by his tone. She also liked the excitement, and his spiced red wine scent. "What's wrong?"

"There's something grave," King Orrin replied. "Today,

the queen remarked that your father will have you married this season. Messengers are riding to prospective midlander lords. He didn't tell you that, did he?"

The trapped feeling closed in around Margot. Belinde, she thought, had meant her remark to be a warning. She was in danger of being forever tied to this place. "I'm sorry to have to give that news," he said. "Also, my lords and I finished today. The last of the men I brought have gone to cut and carry the trees that your father traded for our wine. You and I have no more time to plan. I think I've come up with a way for you to ride with us. It will be risky for you, at first. I'm not happy with it."

"What is it?" Margot asked, the words pouring out in a rush.

"I wish I didn't need midlanders and their wood," he said, frustrated. "It's hard to even ask you to do this."

"Tell me." The plan might be awful; it might be perfect. "I want to hear."

"You could run away after we've left, as if entirely separate from our leaving. Then you could come to where we'll wait for you and place yourself under my protection. It's against my vows to lie to your father, or to ask you to lie. But he and his people are like heathens in some ways, and I, most holy men, don't always explain whole truths to the ignorant, because they don't understand them. You can just go, without lying or explaining. To protect trade, I have to suggest that you never admit that I helped you get away. Once time has passed, you might decide to tell him you're in the westlands. He'll make terms with it. He'll know that no holy man or swordsman would pursue a woman who's chosen a draelan's protection. My draelan and I will look after you. We'll provide all that you need to live. You won't want for anything." He leaned closer to her. "Would you do this?"

Margot breathed in deeply, taking in as much of his spicy scent as she could. He thought her brave and capable enough to run away. He wanted her near him. What she wanted was important to him, too. "There are the demon spirits. How will I stay away from them when I'm on the road alone?"

"I know it's not a perfect plan. I'll have to give you a spelled necklace or belt to protect you, and you'll still have to be careful. It's the best I've come up with, though. I don't know how you've lived this long, listening to the way they talk about you." His voice was rough edged with anger, the kind of anger she'd felt over and over. "I can't just leave you here."

The air was warm between them, all around them. He didn't mean to marry, and maybe she wouldn't, either, because he and she had a kind of bond. He knew what was inside her. He cared about where she'd go and who she was. She wanted to always be this wrapped up, this close and cared for. "I'll do it. I'll run myself, and then we can go to Mawr together," she answered, and she felt she was flying out a window into the world his coming had made, soaring, wings spread wide.

# Four

here was a lot Bird didn't tell anyone.

He crouched, his elbows on his knees, his back against the feast hall's stones. He was in the shadows, not close to the fire. Or the raised king's table, where two holy men ate, alone in the hall except for him. He waited, as he often had in his eighteen years. The men needed to finish eating. Then his father, one of the three best storytellers in the westlands, could enter and speak a tale.

If passersby looked at him, and at this hall, he knew what they'd see. He had his father's hair, long and black, and his father's narrow, patient face. He was his father's apprentice, and wore the storyteller's black tunic and trousers. They wouldn't remember his birth name because no one used it. If they wanted him, they'd call him Bird. Everyone did because they liked the sound of his voice.

They'd also see a hall made of many-sized stones. In the center were two ancient wood pillars carved with scenes of fishing and whaling. A fountain sprang from one wall and ran into a channel that crossed the floor. It reflected the colors in the hall: yellow-orange firelight, gray stone. King Orrin, Demon Spirits' Bane, was still away. He'd gone, as a westlander king went every year, to trade for precious wood. Two of the king's holy men, Holy Glendel and Holy Brandon, were eating fish pie at the king's table and talking. They'd ruled since the king left in late winter. The city of Syllig and all of Mawr had been peaceful, almost as peaceful as the god's sky realms were supposed to be.

Because King Orrin had brought about this peace, he was beloved. Merchants and lords brought him gifts as thanks. The gifts stood around or on his raised table. There was a high-backed chair built of blackwood. There was also a pitcher and dishes inlaid with pearls for his table. Two tall candleholders of rare red silver had arrived not long before. Even the poor left gifts, flowers that stood in buckets by the windows that overlooked the Sea.

Outside, Syllig and Mawr's cities, villages, and countryside were safe. King Orrin had had street lanterns and crumbling buildings repaired. The king's swordsmen now sought out all criminals, not only those who harmed the rich; there was also less danger that a poor man might be robbed of what little bread he had. Thieves, murderers, and pirates—all who traded with demon spirits for forbidden magics like charmed weapons or spells to raise dead souls—had fewer places to hide. Moreover, King Orrin used his magic in ways no one had before. He'd found how to fight the demon spirits' rank winds and blinding lights. He'd taught other holy men to do the same. They hunted demon spirits throughout the land. So anyone could walk anywhere in the city during the day. Anyone could stand on a doorstep and look at the stars during the night.

That is how all saw the castle and Mawr, except the murderers, the thieves, and the pirates. And except Bird.

He shifted, stretching his back. The stones in the wall behind him seemed rubbed smooth by generations of backs like his. He kept his face just as smooth, patient. He wasn't patient within. He saw differently.

The hall used to show no sign of Orrin. Orrin used to be the king's barely acknowledged bastard son. Gawky and awkward, he'd hung at people's elbows. He had always been opening his mouth and spouting opinions. He had always had to insist he knew more than anyone else. He'd boasted when he was right. Back then, Bird had thought most about stories he'd been learning. Sometimes the people in stories, like Gwist the tricky fool and a princess who told the biggest lies in all the westlands, had seemed more alive to Bird than anyone he spoke or sat with. So he hadn't paid Orrin much mind. He'd never had to obey him. Bird missed those days.

As for the gifts—the inlaid pearl pitcher and dishes, the chair, the candleholders, the flowers—Bird imagined taking them down the cliff the castle sat on. He could see himself throwing them into the water one after another. They'd float or sink. Some pearls would scatter. Blackwood would crack. Silver would twist. The Sea would eat the flowers. He smiled.

*The fish took them,* he could imagine saying, if anyone thought to ask him. *You've never seen a fish climb a cliff?*

# Five

argot sat crouched in the mouth of the holy men's tunnel. She'd pulled the door nearly closed. No one would be able to see her, but she could see into the entrance and feast halls. Two long days had passed. Now, once all the lights went out, she was going to meet Orrin.

The feast hall's lights shone steadily through the doorway; of course everyone had chosen this night to sit up late. She stretched one stiff leg, pushing her sack out of the way. It was already packed with her book and the few other things she was taking. She'd splashed her face in the lake for the last time, trying to memorize its murky scent, a mixture of mud, rain, and frog smells. She'd told Belinde she was leaving, and Belinde had wished her luck. The queen had also done a surprising thing. When Margot had said goodnight earlier, her father had said his usual brusque "Sleep well," seeming to suspect nothing. Belinde had kissed her cheek—really kissed her, not the air several inches from her face. The kiss had made Margot want to cry. She hadn't, but the one thing she'd miss, besides the lake, was Belinde.

She didn't want to think of the queen now. She stretched

her stiff legs again. She ran her fingers over the ties on her light summer cloak. She thought of Orrin. Before he left, he'd taken the cloak from her. His hands had brightened, first in lines like veins, then throughout his fingers and palms. She'd watched, amazed; she'd seen rites but had never seen a holy man spell something. Without the help of others, which she'd heard most holy men needed to spell nonmagical things, he'd made her cloak darken. Then his hands had faded. He'd said she wouldn't be invisible, no one could be, but he'd woven in an illusion so that the wool would look more like a shadow than cloth. He'd also woven in protective spells. The cloak would burn demon spirits if they touched it. The hood would keep the spirits' lights from blinding her. She'd have to stay on roads and paths, though. The spirits' magic was stronger in wilder places; they'd break the protection spells if they caught her in a field or forest. Margot put her nose against the wool. Her protection, the spells, made it smell faintly of iron. She was ready. She was going, and not coming back.

The light went out. Margot half rose, then stayed crouched. She tried to imagine the span of time it would take several people to climb the back stairs to the upper sleeping rooms. She shifted, wiggling her numb toes. *Time to go*, a voice inside her urged. *Time to go*.

She was a shadow, not flesh, just a shadow creeping through the dark entrance and feast halls, then the kitchen. The kitchen scrubs lying near the hearth slept soundly. There was the side kitchen door. She slipped out it and into the cool air. The guards on the wall didn't notice her. She was just one more shadow in the night. She avoided their dangerous lights and followed the edge of the castle, walking in weeds. She went around the corner. There was nothing back here but the outhouses and the stream where scrubs dumped refuse. She pulled a corner of her cloak over her nose and mouth to block some of the stink. In the wall, hidden behind the first outhouse, was the siege door. It was the one means of escape if the castle was falling to an enemy. She put a hand against the rough-hewn wood. This door led out. *Time to go. Time to go.*

Beyond the door, outside the wall, were demon spirits. It was dark, and the moon wasn't fully up. This was when they came out. And so? She wasn't going to turn around and go back. Gently, she lifted the siege door's bolt and pulled the handle. She took a step into thick briars. There was supposed to be a footpath. Where was it?

"Who's there?" called one of the swordsmen from the wall above. Margot stopped, stone-still outside, panic rushing inside.

"What is it?" came a second voice.

"I heard something in the bushes."

She should run. No, she should stay still.

"We could go down and check." The second voice sounded reluctant.

"I can't see anything from here. Must be an animal," the first voice answered, then spoke more quietly, as if the second man had walked closer.

Light shone down onto the briars and her bent head. The urge to run was insistent. The light from above showed her the footpath beneath her, a little overgrown with brambles. Her knees quivered with the effort of not moving.

Grasses rustled. The light moved away. She didn't hear talking anymore. She waited until the whistle sounded for the watch to change. Joking voices called to each other in the night. Inch by inch, she moved sideways through the briars and pulled the door shut. A neglected footpath might not be enough to prevent demon spirits from breaking through her cloak's protections. She was going to stop thinking about that. Those on watch clomped to their new posts. She began to creep down the footpath, which led around the wall. She was a shadow, only a shadow.

She kept going. Above her, on the wall, the swordsmen were silent. They didn't notice her creeping below them. The footpath veered into the forest. Margot walked under the canopy of trees. She couldn't see the men on watch any longer, so they'd missed their chance to see her. She halted.

She was away from the wall. Outside it.

The moon was rising, but moonlight didn't reach here except in stray strands. Leaves rustled, hushed, rustled again. Demon spirits could be standing in the places moonlight didn't reach. They could be crouching above, among the leaves. They'd make her their drudge in the underground realm. Or they'd keep her up here, in the places they claimed as their own. They'd make her do awful things for them—steal, kill.

She started forward, stumbling over roots and uneven ground. The road was ahead, all moon-silvered. She pulled a stone that Orrin had given her out of her sack. It was flat and round, and he'd spelled it to cast a warm yellow glow. With its light, she easily got to the road. Her strides lengthened. She should have been more frightened. Instead, she felt she could go anywhere. No wall encircled her, keeping her in.

She had to walk only a few miles. Orrin had left but hadn't traveled far. He and the men with him had gone to see the trees he'd traded for. They planned to make sure the swordsmen and laborers had everything they needed. They meant to examine carts and food supplies. Then, tonight, they were going to stay at a town close by. He and a couple of the others would meet her, by a huge tree he'd said was in the road's center. He'd wanted to be certain she didn't have to walk long alone.

She smiled, remembering his concern. She didn't think anyone had ever asked her "You'll be all right?" so often.

A mile or two took no time at all. She didn't see any other travelers. Some hares startled her, and she gave an embarrassing little shriek. They dashed away, their big funny feet kicking out behind them.

She went farther down the road. It was hard to judge how long she'd walked. She thought she should see the tree soon. Wild dogs in the distance began to call as they had a few nights before, ululating. Just wild dogs howling at the moon. That was all they were. Nothing else.

The howling stopped. She heard footsteps, like an echo behind her. She stopped.

The footsteps continued.

She ran.

The footsteps ran, too. She glanced at a shape running beside her. It was human-like, but gray and shifting, with a coldly beautiful face and wild tangled hair. Margot's cloak protected her as long as she stayed on the road, that was what Orrin had said. But she ran faster. The spirit kept pace with her. A boggy, rotten stench was all around—in her hair, up her nose, on her skin. She felt no wind and saw no lights, but a hand stretched from the spirit. Long, sinewy fingers reached for her shoulder. She swerved. Two more hands—no, three—appeared. They came from three more swirling spirits. She stumbled and realized she was at the road's edge. They were trying to drive her off. She swerved again, this time toward them. Those hands would grab her, touch her. The cloak wouldn't keep them away. They were too close.

She tripped, hitting her knees hard on the packed dirt. Straightening her hood, she scrambled up. The many fingers were nearer, ready to grab her arms.

She dashed around a corner, and the edge of her light showed the road splitting at a massive trunk. It was the meeting place. She held the light higher. The tree stood by itself. Orrin hadn't come for her.

Then a wind spun around her. It twisted like the winds holy men called up as part of rites, but was harsher. It yanked Margot forward to the huge tree, which she grabbed, but shoved the spirits away into the forest. The spirits howled like savage, furious dogs. The wind faltered. The boggy stink rushed past her. Then the wind whipped strong again. Abruptly, the howls fell silent.

The wind died down, and a handful of lights flared, each held by a man who stepped from the forest onto the road. "Margot." One man pushed back his hood to show his silver circlet and blond hair: Orrin. He hurried toward her. "They're gone for now. Are you all right? They didn't reach you?" he asked. His face was weary.

"I'm fine." She let go of the tree. She was damp with sweat, but she was alive. He was here. He hadn't abandoned or forgotten her. "You're hurt?"

"No, a little tired. Thank the god for Meynard; he's the fastest at calling up a wind to carry them away." Orrin nodded back at five other men, two swordsmen in red tunics, two lords, and a holy man. Meynard, the holy man with the long mustache, slumped as though exhausted from using too much magic. "They didn't harm you." Orrin stopped very close to her. He reached out and touched her arm, gently holding her elbow as if to make sure she was really standing in front of him. "You're not hurt at all."

She was transfixed by his light touch. He'd been scared for her, he still was. She felt that warmth again, that feeling of being wrapped together, cared for. "I was just frightened," she replied.

"Mawr isn't like this anymore. We'd forgotten how dangerous night travel can be," said Meynard. He, too, seemed upset. "We should've thought of a safer way, Princess."

"I'm sorry. It's such a short distance. I didn't think they'd come." Worry made Orrin look younger than he was, an awkward boy. Did he fear she wouldn't forgive him?

"It's all right," Margot said. He smiled; he seemed glad because of her words, her forgiveness. "I'm fine."

"Let's go, then, before they come back. You renounce the protection of your father's line?" asked Meynard, as if this was what he'd expect any sensible person to do. He now held on to the man next to him for support. "You put yourself under the protection of King Orrin of Mawr and his city's draelan?"

Orrin smiled wider. His hand still cradled her elbow. Her father had no power or say here. She did.

Margot hesitated a moment. Then she let her answer flow out and alter her life. "I put myself under King Orrin's protection."

# Six

ird didn't like so much sitting. He also didn't like to be inside the draelan guesthouse so often—it was summer. He crouched on a bench, however, watching his father sleep. The fire burned high to keep the storyteller sweating out the illness. Bird sweated, too. He was glad his father was getting better, but he was restless.

He closed his eyes. He thought of roads. They were dusty in the summer, and smelled of horse. The ports were loud with the sounds of boats coming and going. In the countryside, away from the port and shore, were the grapes. Rows of short, spiny trees stood on hillsides and in valleys. Vines draped over them. As summer went on, the clusters appeared. The grapes blushed red and purple. Some tasted so sharp they made his eyes water. Others were sweet, their flesh swollen with juice. At harvest, women picked with their skirts tucked up and their sleeves rolled. Eating grapes always made him think of bare wrists and ankles. Sometimes in his dreams, he lay in a vineyard next to a woman. Her hair smelled of sweat and sunlight. Her skin was sleek and taut like grape skin. When he kissed her wrists, one tasted sharp, the other sweet.

Any other summer, he'd be walking roads past ports and

vineyards. His father would tell stories in lords' manors or, sometimes, in inns. Each morning they'd start on roads again. Each night they'd arrive at a new hall. They might make their way to another of the five westlander kingdoms. In Isdur, they'd eat swan every night. In Lerrow, the old king would drowse while his queen asked for tales of young men and the women they won over. Anywhere, though, they'd hear of Beloved Orrin this and Beloved Orrin that. All the westlander kings were looking more and more to Orrin and his draelan for guidance. Always before, each draelan had made its own rules. Now there was talk that Orrin's draelan should lead the others. So Beloved Orrin would make decisions for all the westland draelans.

Bird climbed off the bench and lay on the floor rushes. He listened to his father's slow, heavy breaths. The fire's heat burned. Bird had felt this hot the previous winter. It had been the night he'd shamed himself, and had realized how little he wanted to be led by Beloved Orrin.

That night the winter before, his father had also been ill. No, he'd been exhausted from using too much magic. Orrin had called for a story. Bird knew the king would rather have sent for his father. Bird was an apprentice and hadn't yet inherited the full storytelling magic; he didn't have the strength for whole illusions. He also hadn't yet inherited all the stories of his line. But he'd learned to tell tales the exact way the old cousin-uncle-grandfathers, as he liked to call even those of his line he didn't share blood with, and his father did. And like every apprentice, he'd learned a handful of stories that belonged only to his line, only to his father and him. Orrin liked the tales his father told and the way he told them. Besides, none of the other great storytellers would be wandering near Syllig. They'd be at the castles where they wintered.

Orrin would rather have called Bird's father for other reasons, as well. When he and Bird were boys, Orrin had trailed after everyone, trying to get them to listen to him. He'd wanted to talk of right and wrong, good and evil. He had schemed, even then, ways to drive off demon spirits. Everyone wanted demon spirits gone, but Bird had wanted to laugh, not hear the half-forgotten prince go on and on. He'd mostly ignored or avoided Orrin. Who had hated to be ignored or avoided. Bird hadn't cared what Orrin hated.

That night, the winter storms were fierce. Bird took the holy men's tunnels to the castle. As he made his way in the dimness, he wished his father no longer wanted to winter here. Orrin's voice and words grated like fingernails scraped against stone; no one called him a braggart, but that was the way he sounded to Bird. Unfortunately, it was futile to wish to winter with another lord or king. Bird's father had always stayed in this castle, and thought Orrin better than many kings. Orrin certainly wouldn't ask them to leave. He liked Tomos Silvertongue, as well as the honor and reputation the great storyteller brought to the city by wintering here. Bird might stay elsewhere once his father passed on, but that wouldn't be soon. He and Orrin had to endure each other.

The feast hall was mostly empty, except for Orrin, Holy Meynard, a few lords and ladies, and some scrubs. The shutters were closed over the large windows to keep out drafts. This made the hall dimmer than usual. It also smelled more like a stable yard; the winds and rains hadn't let up in so long, there'd been no dry rushes for the floor. As Orrin, Holy Meynard, and the rest finished eating, Bird stood to the side. He bowed his head and thought of how he'd rather be out in the storm. He'd meant to slip into the city, despite the blowing cold. He hadn't seen the weaver's daughter in several nights.

He missed her wine-red gown and her curling hair, which fell over his hands as he unbound it. He also missed how she, in a way, told stories. The words she used were plain, but she'd tell about her mother's feud with another weaver and how the brewers' sons stepped on her feet at dances. She'd get him laughing so hard his stomach hurt.

Just then, he'd have liked to be tapping on her window shutters. They'd meet in her mother's dye house beyond the larger city house. It had a jumble of floral and rank scents. At night, it was entirely dark inside. He would have liked to see Elene, to watch her. She preferred the dark. She'd once said it let her stop being the polite, obedient weaver's daughter who would one day be a weaver herself. She could be someone other. After she'd told him, he hadn't suggested a light again. That someone other was startling and fun.

"Storyteller's Apprentice?" Orrin said, sounding as if this wasn't the first time he'd asked.

"Yes, Highness?" Bird tried to seem attentive. The holy man, the various scrubs, the two lords and three ladies were attentive, but that made Bird itch. At least one of the lords and two of the scrubs had spent several years disregarding Orrin. Now they nodded like lap dogs no matter what he said. Was that how he seemed, so two-faced and fawning?

"'The Good King.' That's what we'd like to hear, please." Orrin settled back in his chair, smiling.

There were few stories of his line that Bird liked less. 'The Good King' was boring.

Still, he did as he'd been asked. He told of the Good King, who could walk right after he was born and who talked like a full-grown man by the time he was two. He saved his people from famine. He built a great wall around his land to protect it from southern raiders. He married a woman so fair and wise, the people loved her as much as they loved him.

Despite the pallid words and story, Bird enjoyed the magic. Within him was a place he thought of as a well. He didn't know how deep it was, only that it was there. Without having to close his eyes and try, as he had when he was younger, he felt the magic rising in him. It came up through the well and through him. It warmed his belly, then streamed outward. Once the warmth flowed into his hands, he could feel the magic's running water shape. As the story came from his mouth, the words, or maybe it was simply his mind's vision and desire, made the magic shine in his palms and form an illusion. He shaped the Good King's circlet, gold and smooth. Then he shaped the stone the king's people gave him. It was large, gray, and craggy. It had praise carved in it: *Forever live the Good King.*

He spoke the last word. He let the magic sink. Surprised, he realized that Orrin's face showed displeasure.

"I've seen you tell better," said Orrin. His voice had the grimness it always had when he was angry. "You don't like this story?"

The pleasurable warmth was gone. Bird's forehead, all of him, went hot with shame. Regardless of how much he favored or didn't favor a tale, he wasn't supposed to tell it so poorly that people would look as Holy Meynard and the rest did, disappointed. "I like every story of my line, Highness," he replied.

"You prefer stories where people die of famine? Or tales full of fools? You don't like to speak of heroes and their feats?" Orrin asked quietly. He seemed disgusted. The others examined Bird. The ladies' eyes were like cats', condescending, and maybe amused that he'd been so inept with what they considered a good story. Bird's face was on fire.

"Of course I like heroes, Highness," he said, not mentioning that he liked very few. Others found heroes' goodness and their overwhelming, unmarred triumphs exciting. He found them tiresome. Still, he hated that he'd been so careless and shoddy with one of his stories. And that they'd all heard and seen him.

Bird waited for Orrin to insult him further. The king might even hand down a punishment, a sign Bird would have to wear proclaiming he'd disappointed the king. It'd be shaming, and Orrin would enjoy it. Bird wished his father didn't have to find out.

"It's all right. He's just an apprentice," Orrin said instead, as if choosing, like the Good King, to be generous. The ladies turned their cats' eyes on him and smiled. "You'll know not to make this mistake again. You may leave," Orrin went on, still harsh, but forgiving in the way a better man forgives a lesser man.

Standing there, forgiven, Bird felt as though the ground had shifted slightly beneath his feet. From where he was now, he could more clearly see his future stretching before him. Storytellers gave what was asked of them. The man he might most often have to give to was Orrin. Whom Bird just didn't like. Bird was suddenly overwhelmed with an intense revulsion; he'd have to serve, perhaps for a very long time, someone he'd rather ignore. That was part of what "storyteller" meant. The word was now tarnished. He felt feverish and troubled.

~⚬~

Bird still burned, remembering.

He glanced at his father, who was sleeping. Last winter, once the storyteller had been able to sit up, Bird had confessed about the inept telling. His father's black eyes had made Bird feel no more than five years old, and foolish. He'd said: "Don't falter like that again. No one wants to hear his favorite tale told poorly. Even a common streetcorner tale teller has to remember that." Bird had nodded, ashamed.

Bird looked back to the fire. Despite his shame, from that

moment he'd felt as if there were two of him. One was his father's apprentice and son, who did just as he should. The other, hidden one had this hunger, the kind he'd found in no one else but the cheats, liars, and thieves in Syllig. It was an animal hunger for Orrin to fail as a king, to earn nothing but dislike and ridicule. Though more swordsmen and holy men kept rich and poor safer, though the demon spirits couldn't hunt as they once had, though people were happy, he still felt it, a demanding ache that wouldn't go away.

# Seven

fter leaving the tree and the road, Margot and the others joined the rest of Orrin's men at a small, dingy inn. Inns were for merchants, not nobility, but the midlanders didn't question men coming in late at night, especially not westlanders. The next morning, Orrin took Margot's summer cloak and rewove the illusion. No longer shadowy, the cloak became gray and forgettable. Margot covered herself with it. She liked the feel of the light wool on her shoulders and head, hiding her away. Her father would soon know she was gone, but he wouldn't catch her.

She climbed on one of the pack horses, a gray one whose load had been distributed among the rest. At first she listened for her father's swordsmen as they rode past boys leading mules, farmers wearing wide-brimmed hats, and small villages with their holy men's draelans and market squares. She wasn't used to riding this much and this steadily, and the cloth and leather saddle seemed to grow harder and harder underneath her. As midday came and went, her knees felt as if they were full of pudding. She could barely keep them pressed against the horse's sides. She clenched her teeth, thinking only about staying on.

For days Margot's inner thighs and calves ached so badly they burned. She had raw patches, sores. She held on. She watched for her father's swordsmen. Eyes and burning aches, that was all she was.

She didn't realize the pain was leaving until she woke one morning in a small inn room and found it was mostly gone. She pulled on her stained travel gown and went out into sunshine, feeling she'd been in a haze that had finally cleared away. As they all mounted and rode, she was able to notice things. The land was still familiar looking, full of low hills and forests and streams. The mountains that separated the midlands from the westlands didn't seem any closer. They were purple and jagged against the distant edge of the sky.

She also noticed more, this day, about those riding with her. There were six men. She remembered Orrin had said many more had come across the mountains with him. They were now spread throughout the midlands, cutting trees and hauling them back to Mawr. Of the six men left in the group, two were swordsmen. They wore red, and each had a black wolf emblazoned on his chest, the insignia of Orrin's family, most likely. Two others were lords with simple circlets. Those four rode ahead of her and talked of hunting and fishing. Orrin and Meynard rode behind her. They were talking, too, but in the low voices holy men usually used. No one mocked her. When she heard horse hooves coming toward them, she stiffened. The men also seemed to tense, and they drew nearer to her. The passing riders didn't carry her father's swordsmen, just a merchant in gaudy stripes. Orrin's men joked about him as he rode by; their tense readiness, and hers, disappeared. She felt she already fit among them.

Orrin guided his horse next to hers. His hair was very yellow in the sunshine. "To reach a large village before dusk, we have a hard ride ahead of us," he said apologetically.

"For a change, I'm ready," she replied. He gave his barking laugh. She gave one, too. Hers was different than it had been in Pristanne. It was louder and happier.

The rest of the day, their pace was too quick for laughter. They were careful not to overtax the horses, but often this meant walking and leading their mounts, not resting. Once, they passed fortunetellers. A skinny man who wore his hair short called, "Fortunes told. Don't miss this chance to learn what will come to pass." The women with him wore blue gowns, and red wraps bound their hair. Their faces promised honesty, but their wide sleeves and skirts, Margot knew, hid powders that sparkled, or vials of colored water, all the things they used to dupe and lie. Or maybe that wasn't so. People had been wrong about her. They might be wrong about fortunetellers, too. Still, as the westlanders rode by the women, no one joked that Margot should get down and join her people, and she felt like cheering.

At dusk, weary and dirty, they reached a bigger walled village. Strewn around the village square were stands with steaming cauldrons, gleaming pots, and roaming chickens. Children and dogs tumbled and collided as they chased one other around and around. Women picked over goods. Meynard told Orrin, "I'll go and tell the lord or holy men we don't need a feast or lodging from them. And that we prefer the inn. There's no need for you to do it every time, Highness."

"They'll ask if we have any wine to trade," warned Orrin. "Even if you say we don't, they'll hound you about it. Or demand, as if we were merchants ready to fetch for them."

Meynard nodded and began to ride away. "They ever ask about our lady?" the burly lord, Lord Stephen, asked in an undertone. Margot smiled. She preferred "lady"—they called her this instead of "princess" to help hide who she was—and she loved "our."

"No one has yet. Let's not discuss it in the street," answered Orrin, scanning the village.

They were all watchful as they made their way to the inn across the square. A plump woman met them by the door. She yelled for a boy to take their horses. Then she asked all about the travelers. Orrin told her almost nothing, and they followed her into the inn. Margot walked by the smoky dining hall slowly, watching brooding men and women who laughed too loud. A flute player sat by the hearth and played a tune that danced. A couple of swordsmen stood in the dining hall doorway, village swordsmen; they wore duller browns than a lord's better paid ones would. She kept her hood up. The one missing a finger kept talking to the one with shorn hair as she passed by them. They barely noticed her. She could turn and go by them again, right under their noses. She thought that thieves must feel this kind of thrill as they walked with their secrets under their cloaks.

She didn't go under their noses a second time; she went with the rest up the stairs. They reached her narrow room, and Orrin leaned in the doorway while the others went on. "We'll leave a little later tomorrow. I'd like to go to the week's end rituals at the draelan. Midlanders or no, the holy men won't refuse to let another holy man join them in singing praises to the god," he said. "Rest, and I'll have food sent up, and the bucket of water midlanders call a bath."

"Thank you," she said, a little embarrassed. He'd probably been looking after her for days and she couldn't remember thanking him once.

His eyebrows shot up. "Of course. I'm at your command," he said, with a too-elaborate sweeping bow. "And I'm glad you're feeling better," he added more seriously, then left.

Smiling, she lay down on the bed. She stretched and closed her eyes. She could see how he walked. He'd turn and go down the hallway, his stride long. She could smell him, and feel the way he'd held her arm lightly the night she'd run away. She could imagine him very close to her, so close she could touch his face, his hair, his lips. Her skin was hot all over, and she opened her eyes. Touching his lips might never happen, but then again, it might. Running away and heading west had seemed impossible just a few weeks before, and now here she was.

She sat up, that thought of him still more vivid than the dim little room. Shrugging off her cloak, she took out *The Book of the Sea* so she could hide it. She opened it, just to check that it was all right. What she saw made her straighten.

The page was a familiar one, entitled "Waves," but it didn't look the same. The words shimmered faintly, as if they were written in silver instead of ink. The letter that began the page's first word, a *W*, pulsed like a heartbeat. The waves rose and fell, crashing against a beach. Margot reached out a finger. The page felt as a page should, like vellum, soft and dry.

She leaned close to it. The water was a brilliant azure. The sand and rocks were a rich gray and brown. They looked so real that Margot felt she might fall into the picture and land in the sand. She was suddenly lightheaded, as if she were standing up high. The scent of wild wind surrounded her. Her hands shook.

Slowly, she turned the page. The writing on this page, too, shimmered and pulsed. The pictures were impossibly real. As were those on the next page, and the next. Margot raised her head. The smell of salt water hovered in the room, like the scent of a woman's perfume after she had gone.

They weren't yet near enough to smell the Sea; it was the book.

Margot looked down at the page: "Currents." Its wide, flowing expanse of water ran to the ends of the vellum as if it would rush off and fill the room. Traveling west seemed to have strengthened the book's magic. Her mother, and two other women, as well, knew what this magic was and what it meant. Because of it, they'd also known more about the Sea. Margot traced the lovely pages, then glanced around the room. She was really here. She had really escaped the midlands. She could've been trapped there forever, never finding out what those women had known.

She closed the book and tapped its spine. She didn't want to sleep. She wanted to ride again, to head west and not stop until they reached the shoreline. She laughed at herself. She and her gray horse couldn't ride night and day without falling over.

She thought the knock meant the innkeep had arrived with water or food, but it was Orrin. He held a big bowl of stew and some bread, and asked if she'd like company while she ate. "You brought that yourself?" she said, and looked at the high window rather than at his hair and lips, or his hands.

"I've been telling the innkeeps your head aches. That way they'll stay away and be less likely to remember you." He set the bowl and bread down on the wood table, frowning. "Women innkeeps talk about everyone's business. It's a bad thing there are so many."

"A bad thing," Margot echoed slowly. He had to be joking. He wasn't one of those men who thought women should do nothing but what they were told. "All innkeeps talk a lot." This seemed a lame response; it didn't quite catch what she meant. "Women aren't worse than men."

Orrin sat at the table's bench. "Men talk less," he said, sounding very certain. "Gossip can hurt people, you've seen that, and women gossip more. They said awful things about you."

"Yes, but the men weren't any better," she said. His face took on that grim look that meant he was annoyed. She wasn't explaining well enough. "Men gossiped about me, too," she went on. "All the time."

"I'm not saying they didn't," he admitted tersely. "But name one time men were worse. You can't, can you?"

She could. Boys had called her names like pasty-face and water grub, and worse. She remembered, with a sudden intensity, the lords she'd overheard. All of them had been about thirteen, as she'd been. They'd dared a lean troublemaker to kiss her. They'd offered him all kinds of things—silver, even. He'd said, *I won't do that for silver. She'd taste like a dead fish.* They'd seen that she'd overheard, and had laughed. She'd wanted the ground to swallow her up.

"They all were awful." She wouldn't tell him what had happened, even if doing so would make him understand. "I don't want to talk about it anymore."

He seemed on the verge of saying something, but stopped, and looked away. "Of course." He folded his arms awkwardly across his chest. "I'm sure they were all awful. I know they were. I shouldn't have asked you to speak about them."

She shrugged.

"I hate to be thought wrong," he said, looking at her again. His tone startled her. He sounded almost scared, as if he were telling her something he'd never told another person. "My mother was my father's mistress. He didn't marry her, even after his wife died. The other boys never wanted to admit I was right about anything, as if I was born wrong and would always be wrong."

He was trusting her with this secret. Her. He was showing

her a hidden part of himself, the boy who had wanted everyone to stop laughing at him. "You aren't always wrong," she said to him, to that boy.

"I'm glad you're here," he said.

There seemed to be no floor, no walls, no room. She could live in his eyes, floating in that shade of blue. His hands cradled her face. He was shaking, or maybe she was. Then he leaned forward and kissed her.

# Eight

rrin kissed her lightly, just the barest brushing of lips. They pulled back from each other, but his hands still cupped her face. "I didn't mean to do that," he whispered, not letting her go.

"I wanted you to," she said. She loved the feel of his fingers on her.

"You don't have a father to protect you anymore. I'm supposed to be the one doing it. Meynard will have to protect you from me." He gave a laugh, but it was brief and awkward. He released her.

She had no need for protection. "I didn't stop you. That was my choice."

"Then maybe Meynard will have to protect me from you." This time his laugh sounded more as it usually did. Then his face grew serious. "Even with no wife or children, I rarely have time to sit at the cairns and listen for the god's spirits. I decided years ago not to marry. I didn't mean to court anyone. Now, because of you, I don't know what I mean to do. I need to think. Can you understand?" he asked. "Does that make you angry?"

"No," she told him. Because of her, he didn't know what to

do. He cared that much for her. "I'm glad it happened. That's all."

He pulled up his sleeve. On his forearm was a silver band shaped like a sinuous fish. He slid it off and held it out to her. "Would you take this? It's been in my mother's family for a long time. I want you to have it."

"But it must be important to your family." The fish's head was gracefully arched. The wide tail curled around to splay beneath it. The arm ring looked as if it might really leap and swim. "This is so beautiful. They wouldn't want you to give it away."

"I don't have much family. And I'm not giving it away," he said very quietly. "I'm giving it to you."

The words reached inside and touched her under her ribs. Whether he courted her or not, he didn't want her to leave him.

After that evening she always wore the silver fish; it fit high up on her arm, under her sleeve. Orrin didn't come to her room alone again, but he rode beside her most of every day. They talked a lot of their childhoods, laughing over things that had always hurt before. They also spent a good deal of time in silence, especially when he'd attended morning draelan rituals and seemed lost in thoughts of magic. Margot noticed how easily they recognized each other's wants, handing over food or water with few words. At night, alone, she closed her eyes and felt that one kiss and his fingers on her face. She knew what people did when they were married—or sometimes even when they weren't. *It's like a dance,* she'd overheard an aunt say, *a dance so close you're almost inside each other's skin.* She wanted to be inside his skin. Many holy men didn't think they had time for women; he might decide he didn't. But she still closed her eyes and thought of him.

They rode many, many days. The craggy mountains loomed above. Instead of fields, short gnarled trees and bogs lined the road. The wind was harsher, even though summer was still here. The riders sometimes didn't see more than one small village in a day. The villages' castles and walls were narrower than they'd been in Pristanne. They jutted toward the sky. The people were also taller and narrower. They looked as though they ate less and worked more. "These are borderlands," Orrin remarked, riding beside her. "This is supposed to be part of a midlander kingdom, but their king doesn't think much about it, and it doesn't think much about him."

"It's sort of beautiful," said Margot, watching two girls walking through a bog. They were carrying huge baskets of branches on their backs. She'd never seen girls carry such heavy loads and all the while move with such lithe grace.

"Not if you have to live here," Orrin said. "I did for a while as a child, with my mother. The winter's harsh. Everything is just gray rock and gray sky. It feels like the end of the world." He studied the bog, his face full of dislike. "We lived with a lord and lady, friends of my mother. Their sons, three brothers, collected jokes about boys unclaimed by fathers. They told them at feasts, at the high table."

Margot could imagine him sitting silent while people laughed, cheeks burning, staring straight ahead. "I hated that!" she said. "The laughing when you couldn't get away."

He looked at her rather than at the bogs. "But you've left it behind," he said with satisfaction.

She had. Her father, Isabeau, maybe even a new baby—her father's prize son or just another daughter—and the rest seemed far behind her. Of them all, she wished only Belinde were closer. And the lake. "So have you." She gestured at the other men. "They respect you. Those brothers, they could never do that again."

He rode a little closer and tilted his head so it was nearer to hers. "I stayed with them one night, on the way to the midlands. I was still traveling with many swordsmen and laborers, the men who're now hauling our midlander wood to Mawr. The brothers had to provide a feast, bow low, and give me a seat at their high table. They had to grit their teeth and smile," he said. "It wasn't the most honorable thing to do: I could have stayed elsewhere." His voice lowered. "I don't regret it."

His small, secret revenge wasn't honorable, but she might have done just what he had. "I once ruined my cousin's favorite gown. I splashed mud over it. It wasn't really an accident," she confessed. "I should've felt bad, but I didn't. I still don't."

"Also not honorable," he said, a grin in his voice.

They traveled all day. The sky was darkening to black. They didn't seem to be near a village. They hadn't seen one for several hours. Orrin rode so close to Margot, their feet often bumped. He sat straight and stiff, tense, as she was. She peered into the bogs, watching for the shifting gray bodies and cold, beautiful faces of demon spirits.

The road grew steeper and rockier. Margot saw a lonely shack that tilted to the left in front of them. It had broken walls around it. Lights shone through the shutters' many gaps. They could hear drums and pipes. Hundreds of minstrels seemed to be playing inside the shack, but it was so tiny. The sound had to be made with a kind of magic. The stench of rotting, fetid muck blew toward them. "Walk," Meynard whispered, as his horse veered as far from the shack's side of the road as she could. "Don't say anything. If they notice us, run and don't look back."

Each slow step seemed too loud. Margot's hands were clammy, but the dimness, the feel of her horse beneath her and of Orrin right beside her all gave her a rippling thrill.

"Stop," Meynard said in an urgent whisper.

They stopped. He raised his head as if scenting the air. Orrin was between Margot and the shack. He reached out, his hand closing around her elbow. It felt like part of her body, as if he and she were one person.

"Keep going," Meynard whispered, gesturing them all to ride ahead of him.

She and Orrin stayed together. The music from the shack was louder and more raucous. Their skittish horses picked their way up the steep road. Margot's knees and hands were ready to urge hers to run.

Around the next curve was a village perched on the edge of the incline. The lord's castle was just one thick spike. The wall was made of boulders that looked as though they'd walked out of their places in the surrounding hills. It wasn't far off, but a spirit had only to look out one of the shack's many holes to see them. Sweat ran into Margot's eyes. Orrin's hand gripped her elbow hard.

They reached the wall, and a gatekeeper peered through a slot in it. "We don't open after dark."

"Not for holy men? And a king? Open it. Now," Meynard demanded. They heard the bolts being slid back. Behind them came a cry like that a dog made when it found prey. "In!" Meynard yelled. "Get in!"

The doors swung open, and their horses leapt forward into lantern light. Then the gatekeepers slammed the gate shut and thrust the bolts back into place. Savage, taunting howls came from the other side.

Margot's horse pranced and shied. She pet his neck and tried to whisper soothingly, although her skin was crawling.

"I'll be glad to reach the westlands. Where demon spirits don't do as they please," Meynard said. His lips were thin below his mustache.

Giving the gate a hard stare, Orrin said, "We all will."

Margot would; it must be beautiful, a place where demon spirits had to hide and people were safe outside the walls.

A taciturn gatekeeper directed them to a small inn, the largest building on the square. Margot's horse settled down and began to plod, suddenly exhausted. Margot was still damp with nervous sweat, and was still, though she didn't need to be, on edge.

Once inside the cramped dining hall, Orrin arranged for rooms and food. Margot leaned against the wall beside him, not really listening until she heard him say, "I've heard about that Pristanne princess. Does anyone know what happened to her?"

Orrin was talking to a man standing before him, a swordsman in a blue tunic with the insignia of the village's spiked tower. His lighter skin and dark eyes made him look half westlander, half midlander. "You know she ran off," he said, with the same almost singing rhythm Orrin and his men had when they spoke. "She hasn't been seen, not even her body. Most think the demon spirits found her and took her underground to drudge. The Pristanne king is mourning, but is also furious at her disobedience. If she's alive and returns, he won't take her back. He sent carrier birds to all the midlands with letters declaring her exiled for running off. I hear his people are happy. For years, they've hoped she'd be exiled so she couldn't inherit the throne. You know how they are in the midland valleys about people with westlander blood."

Margot wanted to ask him to repeat all he'd said. She wanted to be sure she'd heard right.

No one was looking for her. No one would try to take her back.

Orrin and his men shifted around her. They left the

swordsman; they climbed the stairs; they whispered congrat-ulations to her and each other. Orrin stood in her door, laughing. He had to leave but kissed her hands, one and then the other.

She stood by her room's fire, still stunned. She was no longer Margot of Pristanne. Her father's name didn't belong to her anymore. Surprisingly, it hurt a little. She remembered a time she hadn't thought of in a long while. She'd been small. She'd sat on her father's lap. He'd wrapped his arms around her. He'd held her tight. She hadn't understood then that that was how you held something you didn't want to let go of. He wasn't going to hold her that way again. Maybe he wouldn't have anyway. But now he never would.

She missed the lake. She couldn't see it again. She couldn't see Belinde. She couldn't show the queen that she, too, had gotten what she wanted.

At the same time, she felt as light as steam rising off water. She was truly free to reach the place where she belonged.

She crouched down and took *The Book of the Sea* from her sack. She opened the book. The firelight made the inscribed names black and the space all around them orange-red. They had a shimmering sheen. She traced them: Ariana Elin of Isles, Tegwen Lassair of Isles, and finally her mother, Maira Alys of Isles of Pristanne. These were her only family now. She traced the names again. Then she turned the page. The next one was blank.

The pictures and writing were gone. Her fingers rushed through the pages, searching for any small picture or bit of writing. All blank, except the last few, where her mother had written about Pristanne. She yanked her hands away from the book.

"It's all still there. It has to be." Slowly, she flipped to the first page again. She read the names. Then she went to the next page.

Faint marks bubbled up. Margot leaned toward them. The marks grew darker, shaping themselves into rocky land and mountains. They also formed walled villages and cities' names, which were written in strange curled letters like the book's title. Roads, also drawn with oddly flourished lines, sometimes crossed, sometimes joined, and sometimes split. They led to the end of the vellum. She turned page after page and realized the book now showed a map of many roads leading west. All of them ended at a shoreline of cliffs and caves, a long stretch of it. The cliffs had paths to stones, rocks, and sand. On the last page, the paths stopped before blue-green water. The water undulated, shining golden with sunlight. Foam rushed up the shore, running over rocks, before pulling back into the heaving body of the Sea. Margot touched the picture. The vellum felt as smooth and fragile as the surface of water. She didn't dare press down on it.

She sat back on her heels. The book held a map that revealed itself now, when she was almost in the westlands. It was leading her to the Sea, as if she'd find or learn something important there. *What was it?*

She stared, fascinated, but a part of her still saw the pictures and words that were gone from the book. They might come back, or not. The book might transform again, or not. The shape of the pages, the cover, the smell, and all the things that were still the same now seemed less familiar. She'd thought she knew the book well. It seemed she'd been wrong.

# Nine

ird sat near the great rocks, a little distance from the throng on the hilltop. Syllig had emptied of its lords and ladies. They stood and admired one another. Beggars ate half-rotten fruits that had been cast off in the port earlier in the day. Spice traders spoke in their odd tongues. Boatmen talked of sails. Their callused hands and feet were cleaner than usual. A jester in yellows and purples walked on his hands as all around him laughed. The bells tied around his ankles jangled. Story-tellers didn't walk on their hands, but Bird wondered if he could teach himself anyway. He liked the ridiculous way the man's clothes flapped and the way his feet stuck up strangely in the air.

His father was near the crowd, surrounded by minstrels in small blue hats. His white-streaked black hair was braided with red string. His narrow face was proud. He wore his black cape edged with red marnloy feathers. Right now, he was Tomos Silvertongue, the Storyteller, rather than a sick, too-thin man. For which Bird was glad. He wanted his father well; it had been a long time since they'd walked together and since he'd sat and listened to his father tell a story. Also, all would now want Tomos Silvertongue to tell tales, not him, so he'd have more freedom to wander away from the castle.

Someone called a toast to the almost dark sky. Midsummer. Since the demon spirits had become less of a danger, the holy men had started holding the rites on the tallest hillside, as they had in the ancient days. Rose petals and grape clusters were scattered on the rocks. The holy men would drone on and on, giving thanks to the god for the season's turning. They'd also give thanks for the grapevines, for their beloved, still absent King Orrin, and for the boats in the port. People would sing. The holy men would call up a wind that would carry the songs, the rose petals, and the grapes to the god's sky realm. Then the fire would be lit and the dancing would start.

In the dusk and lantern light, all the talking, laughing faces were as eager as begging, dimwitted dogs'. They'd soon begin praising glorious Mawr. And glorious King Orrin, Demon Spirits' Bane. Bird spat.

A good man wouldn't smile when one of Orrin's new bridges fell down before it was finished or when Orrin occasionally made a land feud worse instead of better. A good man wouldn't think so often about breaking Orrin's rules. Bird was starting to think he wasn't a good man.

He had no wish to sing or dance through the night. He got up and slipped among the rocks. They were smooth from years of standing in the wind. The cliff face was sheer; he couldn't climb down to the wide stretch of Sea. Not that it would be safe to do so; demon spirits still sometimes grabbed lonely walkers in the dark. He found a boulder to sit on. He could hear the crowd, but only faintly. The waves struck the rocks below and drowned out the excited chatter.

Bird thought of words he liked: *Jape. Stumble. Pearl.* Words had a beauty of their own, even without illusion. They had shadings. *Lost* was not the same when a child lost her button and when a child lost her mother. If a thing was *forbidden,* a man could despise it, or could long for it.

As he longed to see Orrin fail. Bird shifted in his cramped seat. He crossed his arms.

The longing gnawed.

# Ten

he pictures didn't return to *The Book of the Sea*'s pages; the map didn't waver. It was as if the book's magic had somehow sensed that the Sea was nearer to it than before. Margot thought it was leading her to look at and touch, to really learn and know, what she'd read about for so long. She didn't like having to stop for food or rest. She just wanted to go.

But they had to travel slowly. The mountains were rocky, and hard on the horses. Each day, the mounts picked their way along the pass. Each night, the group stayed in one of the thinly scattered villages, which were no more than a family's walled lands. Margot was so impatient she had to remind herself to smile at their hosts.

After a week or so, they started to descend. The air warmed. The land leveled. It was still rocky but more lush. The grasses and vetch were an astonishing blue-green. The earth was, in places, more red than brown. The road grew broader. They approached swordsmen wearing Orrin's colors who stood by a string of huts and a marker. When the swordsmen recognized Orrin, they whooped. Meynard and the rest whooped back: they'd entered Mawr. Margot kept pace with the others but stared. This was Orrin's land, their destination.

She saw no forests. Rocky outcroppings jutted up through the ground. Fields had the only trees, rows and rows of short spiky ones. Grapevines grew over them. Farther along, Margot sometimes saw women. They wore their stained gowns tucked up and their sleeves rolled. They made their way through the rows of ripening fruit with baskets slung on their hips. As they picked, they often sang. The words to the songs were spoken so differently from the way she was used to, Margot couldn't make them out. They made her think of waterfalls.

Every village they rode through had a fountain. Women stood around them, drawing water and gossiping. Children splashed and played in the fountains' stone basins. Men stuck their heads under the falling rush of water and doused their hair. When Margot tossed a cupped handful at Orrin, no one looked sideways at her. They laughed as hard as she did, their voices intermingling with hers. She loved the sound.

Margot and the rest started riding faster now, into the night even. Mawr wasn't entirely safe from demon spirits—people still didn't walk alone after dark—but Orrin had stopped much of the danger. He'd hired many extra swordsmen. They walked the roads and hunted down criminals who had helped demon spirits in return for forbidden magic. The holy men Orrin had trained provided even more protection. They had the strength to fight off demon spirits. The people called them spirit hunters. Margot liked riding without fear as the sky grew more purple and then black. Stars appeared. The low, steadily shining orange ones came out first. Then, high above, thousands of white ones glimmered. Day smells gave way to night smells, like cooling earth and rock. The silver-white moon rose. Margot often didn't want to go inside and leave its beauty.

They stayed with lords rather than in inns. Orrin explained her presence by saying that she was in the protection of holy men; he didn't mention that she was a midlander. They often ate fish or duck. Margot struggled not to spill her food; she was clumsy with the large spoons used here. The lords offered Orrin their best wine, made with secret recipes they jealously guarded. They talked to him about the wood he'd traded for and land disputes they'd had. They discussed weather or grapes. They told about criminals swordsmen had captured. Later in the nights, drummers played their odd flat, oval-shaped drums. Margot and Orrin sat to the side and talked alone. The sound of the others ebbed and flowed around them.

"Did you ever swim?" Orrin asked one night while the rest danced. "They don't in the midlands, I know," he added with scorn.

"Backward. Base. That's what my aunts and cousins said about swimming. Because fortunetellers do it." Margot could laugh about this now. "I do swim. I learned. I'd sneak out." It had been so long since she'd swum. Even baths in the west-lands, where they filled the tubs high, weren't the same. The lake water had cradled her. It had felt alive.

"You learned?" He leaned closer, interested. "How?"

She liked his cleverness; he always wanted to know hows and whys. His closeness was distracting, though. She had to look away from him, at her hands, to remember the answer. "I can float. Anyone can." She shook her head. It had been more complicated than that. "When I stepped into the lake, I could tell the water would hold me up."

He studied her, as if doing so helped him understand exactly what she meant. "How could you tell?"

"Because of the way the water felt," she answered. "It seemed to lift. My legs were so light."

Water in the blood. He didn't say it, but she knew he was thinking it. She was, too. The book hadn't taught her to swim. She'd just known how.

Orrin's high forehead wrinkled. "What's wrong?"

"Nothing. I'm just thinking," she answered, his interest and nearness suddenly too much. She couldn't draw out this thought and look at it clearly. "I want to reach the Sea."

He took her hand and traced each finger, which made everything else disappear, like mist in a hot sun. "We will soon. I hope— I'd like—" He took a deep breath. "Would you pledge yourself to me when we do?"

All the air seemed to leave Margot's lungs. "Pledge? A betrothal, you mean?" Her voice seemed to be coming from somewhere outside herself.

He placed his hand beside hers, close but no longer touching. "Yes."

The color had drained from his face. He was frightened she'd say no. He wasn't just curious or concerned; he was frightened.

She was stars strewn high above, not skin and muscle but sharp white shining lights.

She said yes. His eyes were wide, amazed, smiling. His fingers interlaced with hers. She was fiery, blazing and streaking from one end of the sky to the other.

❧

The next day they headed through craggy hills. Margot kept glancing at him, and caught him looking at her a lot, too. For several days she barely noticed whether they traveled through countryside, village, or city.

She didn't sleep well anymore. They stopped at each day's end. Orrin would stand in her doorway, taking his time saying goodnight. He didn't come in. This was partially because he'd told Meynard everything and Meynard watched over them, telling Margot to go to bed in a bossy, older-cousin way if they lingered too long. Still, some men would have tried hard to get her alone. They would have wanted to brag about how early they'd seen what was under her gown. Orrin didn't, which seemed to make Margot think about him more, the bath water going cold around her.

The book also kept her awake. Its smell was strong, and the map still showed her the way to the Sea. Margot would pace, ready to ride long before morning. Sometimes she'd grow angry at her mother and the other women for not being with her, so that they could explain the book. And, almost more important, so they could tell her how she'd known she could float on the water when she'd touched it. She sometimes thought of what Orrin had said about seal women, fish women, and women who'd drunk Sea water. She wondered if one of these had passed down the book, or maybe even blood, to her. Yet, once the sun came up, the possibility always seemed fanciful and silly. The book had never had pictures or words about any of these kinds of women. If it had come from one of them, surely it would have.

She thought of talking with Orrin, someday, about the book. It seemed unfair that she'd soon advise his boatmen and boat builders but would have to hide the fact that she owned and used a book with magic, as other women had. Maybe he should learn the truth. Maybe others should, too. In her father's castle, she'd had to lock away most of what she knew. Now, what she could say and do seemed as limitless as the sky.

Days dragged by. Margot realized one afternoon that the grape leaves had begun to turn yellow and brown at the edges. A group of Orrin's swordsmen joined them on the road. A chilly breeze blew, bringing with it an unmistakable smell. It was stronger and wilder than the book's. Margot leaned forward in her saddle.

"This is it. This is Syllig, the capital," said Orrin, pointing at a tall wall ahead. "Careful, Margot, you'll fall off your horse."

Margot adjusted herself a little. Wind streamed past her, full of salt and sweetness and other tastes she had no name for. To their left was a gap between two cliffs. Through it, beyond it, was water that rose and fell like the back of a huge dancing animal. The water was so long and wide she couldn't see its end. Its surface caught the roses and golds of the late-afternoon light and glowed. The Sea.

Then more cliffs blocked that glimpse. Margot sat back, disoriented. Shapes before her seemed unfamiliar for a moment, until she realized that they made up a wall, gatekeepers calling a welcome, and buildings. At first, there were only squat lines of crowded dwellings or shops. Their roofs were flat, not slanted like those in the midlands. The road was narrow. It was paved with stone. The Sea smell mixed with odors of horse droppings and rotting kitchen scraps. To avoid the horses, people scattered, some waving and some intent on their errands. Many faces were wind chapped. Then the road broadened and sloped upward. The buildings grew larger, with walls and towers. Margot kept looking left, down alleys or side roads. It was there. Around one of these corners or twists had to be another glimpse.

"You'll see it again when we reach the castle," said Orrin, urging his horse forward as if he shared her impatience.

Margot gave her horse more rein and caught up to Orrin. The slope of the road increased. The men around her talked with excitement about wives and children they hadn't seen all summer. Meynard joked about never leaving the draelan again. The buildings thinned, and bracken and stones stretched to either side. Margot raced forward with Orrin.

They saw the castle at last. Its weathered gray stone looked old and smooth. It seemed almost part of the slope. Four towers rose from its corners, rather than the two many castles had. The rounded door swung open as they rode up. They slid to the ground and brought their horses through the entrance into a center courtyard. Two cooks stood there, and many young and old scrubs. A tangle of women and children with ribbons the same red and black as the swordsmen's tunics rushed over. One lady wore a gown that was a shade of bright purple Margot had never seen before. She hugged one of the lords. A couple of gray-robed holy men hailed Meynard. They all bowed to Orrin and called welcomes. A part of Margot imagined them going silent when they noticed her. She imagined them whispering and taunting, turning away. She breathed in the damp, thick air. It filled her and left a strong salty-sweet taste in the back of her throat. These people wouldn't taunt her—no one had for months. All the same, she didn't want to meet them now. The Sea was so close.

"Come on," Orrin said. He took her hand and led her through a side door. They crossed to the hot, empty high-ceilinged kitchen, which smelled strongly of fish.

"Where are we going?" Margot asked, half smiling; she thought she knew.

"Don't you want to finally stand next to the Sea?" he said, and led her through a hallway, then into the feast hall. There was a fountain right across its center. Water sprang from one wall and ran in a channel along the floor. It flashed with candlelight. Huge shutters were open, revealing a wide door with large windows on either side, all framed by smaller colored panes of glass. Margot looked out. Far below were rocks and water, dancing, feral water. She reached the doors before Orrin.

They went out, past a stone wall and a gate to a flower garden. Then they rushed down a set of steep stairs carved into the rocky cliff. Margot adjusted her sack. Her book bumped against her back. It had led her and she'd arrived. *You're here,* the waves seemed to be saying. *You've come.*

They reached the bottom. Orrin went down a short slate path that lay among the rocks and boulders. The wind pulled tendrils of Margot's hair loose from their pins. She started to laugh.

Orrin stopped where the path met the beach. He gestured as if everything before him were a huge present for her. "Isn't it magnificent?" he asked.

The Sea was everywhere. It stretched around them in all directions except the one from which they'd come. It was vast and glorious. She pulled off her worn boots and ran forward. Cool water pushed and pulled at her ankles. A shiver went up the back of her heels and legs.

"Absolutely, absolutely magnificent," she called to him. "Come in."

He stopped at the water's edge. "What are you doing? You're wet," he said, but his tone was pleased.

"I just wanted to feel it," she said.

"And what does it feel like?" he asked, interested, as usual, in those whats, hows, and whys.

Laughing again, she said, "Home." She wanted everyone, everything to hear. "My home."

# Eleven

argot left the stone draelan guesthouse where she slept. The air was wet and heavy, as it had been both mornings since they'd arrived. She scrambled over the low slate wall that ran around the draelan. She'd seen a stairway near here, similar to the one outside the castle. She had to get down to the Sea.

She'd slept much of the last two days, but this morning, the map in her book had changed. It showed the roads that meandered across the westlands, as before. Also, as before, it showed the shoreline, the paths leading down to the waves, and the small, scattered westland islands. It still didn't show the Western Isles, which were far west and a long, hard journey away. The map's color was different, though. It was a shimmering gray, like the fog when the sun began to rise.

Also on the map, in the Sea, a brilliant white light shone. Its glow wavered, as if it were coming from deep underwater. It pulsed like a beacon, a marker.

The map didn't reveal what the light marked. But the book might change again and show her more. The map might not be complete. She was going to look at the Sea in case the light was in the water right now.

She found the stairway, which was all stones and pale green lichen. She began to go down quickly. It started to meander to the side. Maybe she couldn't reach the water this way. She'd have wasted time if this didn't lead to the shore. She clambered around a boulder, hoping to see the path arch back down. It did. She went on.

Close to the bottom, the path leveled out. Margot walked toward the last steps. Then she almost leapt out of her skin. A man with long braided black hair and a black cloak was sitting on a rock. His cloak had red marnloy feathers, but only at the collar: he was a storyteller's apprentice.

"What are you doing?" she demanded. He must have heard her approaching. He could have said something.

"Lady." He rose and bowed. "I was sitting." His voice had a lovely lilt to it, but was also laughing at her.

"I mean, why didn't you call out and let me know you were here?" she asked, exasperated.

"I'm sorry, Lady. I didn't mean to startle you. Still, you startle well." His tone had been more sincere, but was now a little mischievous. "I don't think I've ever seen anyone jump that high."

"Thank you," she said stiffly, although it was silly to be annoyed. Some storytellers teased everyone. They liked best to tell stories about tricky Gwist, who made even holy men and kings look foolish. Only hard-mouthed swollen-heads didn't laugh at such teasing and stories. "I'll try to jump higher next time, Storyteller's Apprentice," she said more pleasantly.

His mouth quirked into a smile. "Just Bird. That's what I'm called," he said, bowing again.

The man's master would tell the tales, but he might stand up once or twice. He probably could make a hall roar. "I hope you'll tell stories soon," she said, ready to go down the last steps.

His narrow face was suddenly very still, as if she'd said something insulting. "You might hear one from me. The king calls, and I serve, Lady." His lilting voice had an angry kind of laughter in it. "If you're trying to reach the shoreline, the new draelan path is easier. It's over there." He pointed away from the castle. "Nearer to a couple of the port paths." Then he turned and started climbing up the hillside.

Taken aback, Margot didn't answer. Maybe he wanted to tell stories more often than Orrin asked him to. Or maybe he was just mean-tempered.

After a curious glance at him, she went down the final steps. She began looking out into the water. It was calm right now. The foam played tag with itself up and down the shore. The fog glinted as it had in her book, the sun just starting to burn through. She squinted but didn't see a light, just a few mounds that might be bare, rocky islands. Where was it? What did it mean? A strong gust of wind blew around her, grabbing her hair, making her eyes tear up, filling her. She leaned into it, searching for the beacon-like brightness.

She paced and looked. Down one way, back past where she'd come from, she could see boat masts. That was the beginning of the port. The other way was studded with rocky outcroppings that would more likely hide coves. Orrin had said there were private coves nearby, one for men to swim in and one for women. She wanted to go in the women's, but she wasn't sure she'd like swimming near other people. Now wasn't the time to go anyway. The book's light had been in the open water, this open water.

"Margot," a voice called from above and behind. "What are you doing?"

She turned, and Orrin leapt off the last stairs from the castle. "You finished early," she said, delighted; he usually wasn't able to get away before dark. Maybe they could have a whole stretch of day to themselves. She almost mentioned the light, then realized there was no way she could without speaking of the book. "I'm walking," she replied, scanning the water.

"We were going to walk later," he said. He sounded as if he was accusing her of forgetting.

Stung by his tone, she looked back at him. "I know that. I didn't forget."

"But you want to walk now." This, too, sounded like an accusation, as if she'd forced him out here.

Margot thought of how Isabeau had often made men follow her by simply going before they were ready. She hadn't intended to seem like Isabeau. "You don't have to come. It's all right. I can stay out by myself," she told him, feeling bad.

"You want me to leave you?" he demanded.

She was saying everything the wrong way. "That's not what I mean. I was just going to walk alone. Like you walk alone."

"Not often," he objected. "I barely have time to come out with you, much less on my own."

Margot paused. He couldn't mean he didn't want her on the shore without him. "So I shouldn't be here by myself?" she asked slowly.

He looked away, as if he *had* meant that but could hear, as she spoke, the unfairness of it. "You can. Of course," he said, but his shoulders hunched; she thought he'd found it hard to say. He climbed the rocks near them. "Come up. Come look."

Part of her wanted to balk and turn away. She'd been answering all wrong, but he really wanted her to be in when he was in, and out only when he was out. "Look at what?"

He spread his arms wide. "At this. The Sea." he said, his voice softer and a little apologetic. Her annoyance lessened; he knew he'd been mistaken. She scrambled up the rocks as he gestured ahead of them and said, "What do you see out there?"

The vast blue-gray water stretched to the misty horizon. It was her mother's love, lost forever. It was her heart, swelling and crashing. "Everything," she said, unable to explain.

"What's within it, do you think?" he asked. "Underneath the waves."

"Underneath?" She thought of the map's wavering light, shining like a beacon. She thought of the pictures the book had shown her, the currents with different swirling paths and the underbelly of a wave. "A lot. I wish I could see it all."

"Sometimes I think I can almost glimpse down past the surface," he said with longing.

He'd never told her that before. "What's there?" Margot asked him.

"I don't know." He shook his head. "My mother, like yours, had water in her blood, but only in a weak way. Every so often she saw odd colors and lights in the Sea."

Margot drank in these details. What else had his mother seen? When he walked in the sand and watched the waves, what did he see? Had he seen the light her book's map had shown her? Did he know what the light was? She scanned the water, searching for it, and tried to find the right way to ask.

"You were here and I had to be inside, so I was envious. Sometimes I'm envious of what you know. My mother's gift was weak, but I don't even have that. I want to understand what's beneath the waves." He clenched his jaw with frustration, as if his wanting to understand how and why pushed him hard when he looked at the Sea. "I'm sure there are things in the water we know nothing about. Maybe creatures with magics we can use for healing, or magics that could make our boats stronger and faster."

She couldn't think of uses and creatures the way he could.

Looking out, she could imagine only glances, possibilities. Beneath the surface might be tiny, delicate footprints or flashes of color she could see out of the corner of her eye. The light might have huge round spokes. It might be a narrow beam. Or it could be only the beginning of a change in the map, unfinished and meaningless for now. She had that same longing to know he did; it was an almost painful tightness under her collarbone. But the book was her guide. She looked sideways at him as he stared at the water.

The book was magic and she was a girl, a woman. Her mother had kept it from her father. The other women had kept it a secret. Now it was hers alone. All the same, Orrin wasn't her father, and he loved water as she did. He, more than anyone, might understand a girl could own a magic thing. Or he might not; he was a holy man. Also, if she decided she could show the book to him, would its magic make it seem like any other book? It had always had that way of hiding when others were near. Would Orrin then think she was a liar? "You shouldn't envy me. I don't know much," she said. Right now, she knew very little, not even whether she should try to tell him her secret.

His mouth eased into a smile, as if he didn't agree but wasn't going to argue. She was glad of both the smile and the silence. They didn't insist she decide or explain anything.

They started to walk again, first with their eyes on the water. Then Orrin began hurling stones, trying to hit rocks far ahead of them. "Wait, I'll get it this time," he kept saying. His aim was good, but the rocks were far. He hit them only once. Margot kicked stones instead. The game was simple and stupid, just swift, hard kicks, cheers when a rock went farther than the rest, groans when one didn't. If she played quickly enough, she thought only of the next rock and not of why the light hadn't appeared.

Orrin brought up their betrothal feast. He wanted to choose a day in the next month, and the wedding for a month after that. The wait was meant to prove that she hadn't arrived here pregnant. He had a strong sense of honor about this, stronger than hers. She'd had cousins who were pregnant before their weddings—before their betrothals, even. People only whispered until the woman wore a wedding band and then seemed to forget. Still, she found his sense of honor sweet.

After a while he stopped. "I should get back. Do you want to come?" he asked. "Or will you stay out here and walk alone for a while?"

She stared out at the water, the fog now just a slight haze. She felt the longing to understand under her collarbone again. It had wound into a knot, but she couldn't make the light or an explanation for it appear. Another look at the map might help. "I'll come up with you."

Smiling, he nodded. She suspected that he was still envious that she had more time to walk the shore than he did; he seemed a little too glad she wasn't staying out alone. She let him think he'd hidden it. Starting to run, she called back, "Let's race."

Orrin beat her to the steps, but not by much. They climbed up to the castle. The feast room smelled of Sea. The windows let in rectangular shafts of sunlight. Young brown-haired twins, the cook's sons, were propping open the windows. Orrin had only a few distant cousins, who didn't live near, so there wasn't the endless family she'd had to endure in Pristanne. The lower tables were full, as they were every day, of men and women waiting to talk to Orrin. At one near Margot, two women, weavers in finely spun skirts and strange hats that looked wrapped onto their heads, were talking about the lady who hadn't paid them the silver she owed; they wanted Orrin to pass judgment against her so the swordsmen could collect the silver for them. There was also a smell that gave Margot a tickle in her throat: a merchant must have just passed through with pungent spices for the hot wine. A swordsman called out, "King Orrin, Demon Spirits' Bane," and everyone rose and bowed. Margot looked out the half-open windows at the Sea, then turned to say goodbye. She'd return to the guesthouse and her book.

One of the swordsmen had led a man to Orrin. The man wore a brown tunic with a black ship embroidered on it. He held a wide-brimmed hat in his broad, scarred hands. Several other men hung behind him as he told Orrin he wanted to ask help of the lady. He said it as if it were a name: the Lady. It took Margot a moment to realize he meant her.

"One of my boat builders, Master Ildorson," Orrin said, introducing the man. "Will you hear his question?"

Orrin had said people would ask her advice. Except she hadn't expected anyone to come to her in the feast hall, the way they'd come to a king for help. She didn't know much about boats or about boat builders. Wood floated, but how did they make so much of it float when it held all those barefoot men and stacks of goods? She might not know the answer to Master Ildorson's question. "Of course," she said, her voice falsely certain.

They went to the high table. She and Orrin sat in his chairs. The boat builder made sure his men were silent behind him; then he said, "You know the hull eaters, Lady? They eat the boat wood. They're small." He held his thumb and forefinger just a tiny space apart. "Like a worm or a grub, but with a hard, narrow shell on their backs. They attach to the ship while you're at Sea and start chewing. If there are too many, you have to put into port and try to scrape them off. But they burrow in." He shook his head with disgust. "Mudflower oil used to kill them. Now they've changed. It doesn't even make them sick. We've been burning them, but we lose a lot of the hull when we do that.

"What else might drive them off or kill them?"

Margot felt a moment of blank stupidity. Others in the feast room—the group of men holding thick rope nets, an herbalist with a curled snake emblazoned on his tunic, lords and swordsmen—had stopped talking to listen. The boat builder and the men behind him wore grave, hopeful looks. Orrin watched her, and his face held no doubt that she knew the answer. She was a fraud.

Then an image came to her of a small brownish grub-like creature with a ridged shell. It had been in her book. She thought it had been, although she couldn't remember the shape of the words telling about it, the way she could for whirlpools or waves. "The creature's also called a raadaulck," she said. "I think."

"Raadaulck." The men all tried the word out on their tongues. "A name we haven't heard for it."

The creature had to have been in her book. A name like that wouldn't just pop into her head. "It needs salt, but too much shrivels it. Flame-weed oil poisons it." Margot remembered the drawing of flame-weed now, with its profuse jagged leaves. She knew this; they didn't, but she did. "I think flame-weed grows in bogs."

"Salt. That's costly. But the flame-weed is common on those little islands to the north, between here and the Far North's peninsula," one of the men behind Master Ildorson said in a quick, eager voice. "I know a man who lives out there—"

"You could take the island hopper," Master Ildorson interrupted, "and pick two others to go with you. We could have some before dark."

She had made this come about, the excitement and eagerness. Without her, it wouldn't exist. She was the cause of things, like rain or fair weather.

The boat builder bowed low before Margot. "My thanks, Lady." Then he touched her hands lightly and murmured, "Blessings on you and on me."

She didn't move. This was what people said when they touched the cairns made for the god's spirits, in hopes of receiving the gift of good luck. Each of the men did it, though her hands were too large and long to be pretty, and they didn't have any gift. Master Ildorson's eyes held strong belief; she couldn't take back the luck he thought he now had.

"You see," Orrin said just to her. "You know a lot that will help us. Look, one of my boatmen is coming in the hall. He'll ask you something, too, I bet."

As a sun-weathered man stopped to talk with the boat builder, she gave Orrin a nod, exhilarated but unsettled. In Pristanne she'd often been ignored, left on her own. Here she never would be.

# Twelve

ird walked through Portside, a part of the city he used to avoid. The streets were narrow, and boys running messages kept bumping him. Cats and dogs fought or stole from the rot piles. Women sitting on doorsteps and mending nets gossiped about the laborers and swordsmen who'd arrived from the midlands with wood that Orrin had traded for. The docks were near, a short walk to his left. Voices shouted orders, and water slapped boat hulls. Gulls fought over scraps, their ruffled feathers and bright eyes making them look like plump merchants. He breathed Portside's distinctive smell: salt, fish, and mud, with a strong underscent of rot.

He passed spice traders from the southern reaches who wore earrings in both ears and had red-brown skin. Their hands were stained yellowish from their spices. The boatmen from the Far North had strange-colored hair, reddish orange. When Bird brushed close to them, he could smell horse, which was what they bred and traded. A young, shaggy-haired urchin spun until he was too dizzy to stand. The small boy fell down, laughing so hard his belly jiggled. Farther on, Bird saw a woman who must have been from the westland islands, which were little more than bare rocks in the Sea. She had a floppy hat pulled low over her face, and a worn gray gown. Her braid hung down her very straight back. Her basket was full of eggs and fish: she must have come off her island to trade. She walked more like a swordsman than a woman, taking long strides.

The buildings were full, overflowing with anything and everything. Poorer merchants sold wares through open windows. Boatmen stood in the doorways of inns. They drank and called jokes to friends on the street. Bird knew, without having to see, that many of the buildings' stairways and rooms held people trading in forbidden goods. Portside was the place to get knives spelled with forbidden magics and herbs that made men both sicken and crave to eat more. Orrin had repaired Portside's lanterns. His swordsmen walked its streets. But despite his attempts at improvement, it was still the dirtiest, most dangerous part of the city. There were too many narrow alleys, back stairways, and rooms hidden behind rooms. Bird had started to walk these streets each day; Beloved Orrin, so far, was failing here.

Bird turned onto a street he hadn't been down before. It was so narrow that he almost had to step over some of the women mending nets. A swordsman, the third of the day, stopped him to ask his route and business. He gave the same answer he'd given the other two, saying he'd come to visit a friend and would then return to the castle. This one, like the others, didn't question him closely after he mentioned the castle. Or maybe it was just that Bird was good at lying.

He kept walking. Elsewhere Orrin thrilled everyone. They loved him and all he did. Here, in Portside, less had changed. Orrin's defeats seemed to glimmer all around. Bird could see them out of the corner of his eye. They gave him a more alive feeling in his chest.

Abruptly, he realized that dusk had arrived, which meant

he should get back. He kept walking. He'd go soon. Just not quite yet.

Bird turned down a street that was dead silent. He stopped. The buildings on either side were blackened, but no street-side fires burned in the fire pits. Shutters were closed over all the windows. The sounds from the street behind him—talking and yelling—those sounds, too, seemed to be hushing suddenly. A sense of foreboding settled over him.

He saw a glow and then a flash of lights around the next corner, coming from the direction of the market square. A demon spirit must be in the city. Behind him, a few people went by on the street that crossed his. They walked swiftly, heading for refuge. He should hide in a doorway or around a corner. Not here, though—closer, where he could see.

He took an indirect route through the alleys, avoiding two streets where swordsmen often walked. Even before he reached the end of the third alley, he could see the lights flaring again. He crept the last few feet. He left the alley's mouth, stole across the walkway, and squatted behind the low wall that enclosed the square.

Four spelled streetlights gleamed from tall crooked buildings. The demon spirit across the square was gleaming as well. It had the form of a man, but its cloak, arms, and legs were misty. Its tangled hair and ruthless face had a white sheen to them. It stood motionless, head tilted, studying its prey as if waiting for some sign. Or maybe it was playing cat and mouse. The air, like Bird, seemed breathless, waiting for the strike.

The prey was a holy man who Bird doubted was a spirit hunter. He was small and elderly. He was behind the arched fountain. He was what could only be called cowering. Even in the poor light, Bird could see sweat dripping down his face. Bird understood fearing the spirit. It would try to blind the man or drag him to the underground realm; he'd never again be free or feel the sun. Facing it must be worse than any night terror. Yet this was the center of Syllig. Hundreds of eyes were watching at shutter and door cracks. Several messages had probably been run to the draelan. The holy man only had to hold the spirit off until his brothers arrived. That was all. Instead, he hunched, as if trying to make himself as small as possible. A part of Bird hurt for him. A part found him pathetic.

The spirit lashed out. Its face and hair brightened. They shone in the growing darkness. A wind spun through the square. It brushed roughly against Bird as it passed, stinking of bog and sewer. Bird gripped the stones in front of him and gagged. The holy man brought up his hands. They flared with magic, but Bird felt no answering wind. It must have risen only around the man, who grunted and staggered but wasn't pulled toward the spirit.

The spirit's face dimmed. It sidestepped around the square's edge. The holy man skittered so that the fountain was still between him and the spirit. Bird saw the spirit grin; then it tipped its head back and gave a long, wild, triumphant cry. Its savagery had a kind of beauty.

Bird found the spirit's behavior bewildering, though. Mawr wasn't a place where a spirit could stand in a market square and taunt a holy man, then escape. Great heroes from ancient days had written in their histories that the demon's underground kingdom was vast, with villages and countries. Was this spirit from far off underground? Did it not know about Mawr? Or was it simply confused or broken, so that it didn't understand that it could be beaten?

Then wind sprang up, like a winter storm screeching in to pound the coast. There were many winds, actually, from all around. They knocked Bird against the stones. He gripped the wall hard as they scraped and battered him.

The demon spirit fought, teeth bared. Its stinking wind spun back around the square. Lights flashed from its fingers; they were so bright Bird hid his eyes. The other winds tore past Bird's face. He peered through mostly closed eyelids and saw the spirit's light rip apart, then flicker out. The spirit rose above the street lanterns and into the dark sky. The winds bore it high over the buildings; they'd drop it in some abandoned field. It howled with fury. Watching a spirit's defeat had once transfixed Bird with astonishment. Now, instead, he was transfixed with resentment. He didn't want to watch what would happen next, but he couldn't look away.

The winds died after several moments. The holy men went to their brother and helped him up. Shutters opened. People leaned out, merchants in their eye-catching reds and yellows. They cheered and touched their sweeping hat brims with respect. The women took the dried flowers they wore in their hair and tossed them down. The spirit hunters smiled. They waved. The youngest even strutted.

Here was one more victory for Orrin. It would be added to all the others, another proof of Orrin's goodness and rightness.

Bird wanted to stand and say that everything wasn't all shining, good, and right. One merchant's wife offered flowers but didn't toss them, so that the young strutting holy man would come close to her. The oldest holy man waddled, his chest puffed out. Orrin, later, when he heard of this fight, would speak of it endlessly. He'd never miss a chance to boast.

Why must Orrin and his victories always shine? Why did no one else want to hear of a merchant's wife's illicit longing, a holy man's silly duck walk, Orrin's bragging? Or maybe Bird imagined all the haze, the silliness, the shadow in such victories. Maybe, since no one else saw them or asked to hear of them, they weren't truly there.

# Thirteen

argot sat in one of the feast hall's chairs, as she had most of the day. The fire's smoke had a pitchy, burnt-earth scent. The fountain sang its song of falling water. Beside her, Orrin and Meynard talked of the midlander wood that had all finally arrived. Even though the pictures were gone from her book, they were with her, inside her, as were the book's oddly shaped letters and the words they had made. She'd opened her mouth and the words had come out for the people who'd walked to the table, one by one.

People still wanted to talk with her. Among the swordsmen and holy men stood an herbalist who held a basket of vials. Fishermen in stained tunics gossiped with a plump old woman. Margot had to speak with them. She also should go see if the map had changed to show her more. Weariness suddenly dragged at her shoulders. She liked the feel of it. In Pristanne, she'd always been so useless.

As Meynard left, Orrin leaned on the arm of her chair instead of his. "You're tired," he said. "More will line up in the morning, and my holy men want to meet with you as well. You don't have to have the swordsmen bring anyone else over tonight." He handed her a glass of dark red wine. "Would you like a story?"

She drank the wine, which she was starting to recognize as Orrin's favorite. It had a peppery taste, and it warmed her throat and stomach. She'd already slipped away several times to look at the map. And there'd be more questions to answer every day. "I'd like that," she said.

"A story!" Orrin called, then said to her, "Which one do you want?"

As she considered, a man rose out of the shadows. He'd been sitting away from the tables, on the floor. She was surprised to see Bird; she hadn't realized he was in the hall. His narrow face was smooth, but something about the way he tilted his head made him seem sullen. "I'm here, Highness," he said.

Orrin made a small noise of dissatisfaction in the back of his throat. "Your father isn't well?"

"An herbalist gave him a draft. I'm sorry, Highness. There's only me." He bowed his head, again doing exactly what he should. His shoulders and back, though, were absolutely straight, as if he resented bending his spine for Orrin.

He didn't like Orrin. That was why he'd been angry when she'd said she hoped he'd tell tales soon. Margot no longer wanted to hear him. "We don't have to have a story," she said.

"Well, it won't be much compared to what his father can do. He's still an apprentice. I try to be patient with him, because his father is the best storyteller in the westlands, but he doesn't like to stand up for me," Orrin said, just to her. He spoke with a slight edge. "He was good at pretending I didn't exist when I was the king's unclaimed son."

"He wishes he could ignore you as he used to?" she asked, studying Bird's stiff back and too impassive expression. He was like her cousins, who would have hated to see her at this high table, respected. She wasn't going to laugh with him again.

"He's always polite, but he disappears a lot. My swordsmen have told me he wanders in the city or among the rocks," answered Orrin. He was smiling, but his tone still had its edge. "He'd rather hide than speak tales for me."

Margot finished the wine in her glass. She didn't want Bird in the hall, but saying he could go would make him happy. "I really want a story. I think he'll have to tell one," she said to Orrin.

"Not honorable," he whispered near her ear. "Getting back at people that way."

"Absolutely not," she whispered back. "But fun."

"So what story will you have?" Orrin asked so everyone could hear. He looked as though he was trying not to smile.

She poured more wine, noticing she was already light-headed, and considered. Bird would probably most hate to tell his favorite stories for Orrin, like one about tricky Gwist. "How about 'Gwist and the Pirate Hoard'? Is that a tale of your line?"

Immediately, Margot knew something was wrong. All she could hear was the fountain. Every eye was on her. Bird's impassive expression disappeared, replaced by a fleeting grin that showed the gap between his front teeth. Then the impassive expression returned. Orrin took her hand and shook his head. "She isn't from here. She doesn't know, and I seem to have forgotten to tell her." He laughed. Everyone else laughed. Margot's face was on fire: she couldn't figure out what he meant. "No story tonight, Bird," Orrin said. The apprentice left the hall.

Orrin drew her up, bowing. People bowed to her and him. They murmured as if about a joke. He led her to the windows. She followed, perplexed. Once they were out the door, in the dark and wind, Orrin said, "I'm sorry. I should have told you. I didn't think of it. I didn't mean to embarrass you."

The salty wind cooled Margot's cheeks. The sky was black and full of stars. She realized she was holding her glass and took a sip. This didn't make the events in the hall clearer. "I understand that, but what did I do?"

He started walking, his fingers intertwined with hers. "Gwist fools lords, kings, and holy men. He steals and lies. The stories make us laugh, but real thieves don't. They let demon spirits in our walls, and they trade for forbidden magics. So our tale tellers no longer tell stories that make thieves into heroes. They don't encourage anyone to lie or steal or kill. It's one of the changes I made to drive out the demon spirits. In another generation, no one except the storytellers will know those kinds of tales exist. Maybe they'll even forget. Ridding ourselves of those stories has helped make Mawr a better place. Now we can travel the roads more freely. We can walk in the night, see the stars." He squeezed her hand gently. "You're not angry at me?"

"No," she said, liking the way his voice came through the dark to her. The wine made her tingle all over. The Sea beat out its rhythm against the rocks. This place was so wonderful, although she'd never laugh at Gwist again; it would be as though he had died. "No one hears those stories here? Ever? Do people miss them?" She bet Bird did, and that he resented Orrin for this, too.

"Why miss hearing of thieves and murderers when you can walk free at night?" he asked, a smile in his voice.

"True. Who'd say: I want the thieves and murderers back? And please, bring back the demon spirits, too." She couldn't stop laughing at this.

He put his arm around her and kissed her neck as they

walked. Stars. Dark. Wine. The edge of his teeth on her skin. She didn't need stories at all.

◦⌁◦

In the morning, Margot pulled out her book, but the map was the same. She walked to the Sea, but there was no light in the water. She paced. Her thumbs tapped against her thighs. Then she went into the feast hall's dim coolness.

The hall already held people waiting to speak with her. Orrin was in the draelan, so she sat by herself. The men and women came to her table and eagerly asked questions. She thought less about the light as she talked. Instead, she remembered pictures and words that had once been in her book. She could see them in her mind as she spoke of Sea plants and red dyes. They hung there as she talked of how to better shape boats and of whether there were richer whaling waters farther south. The day flew.

The sunlight coming from the windows was orange and rose when a tall, lovely lady approached the table. She had coils of brown hair and smooth skin. "I've tried many things, Lady, but haven't found what I need," she said in a steady undertone. Her folded hands were still, but her eyes were hungry. "What in the Sea will stop old age?"

"You're looking for something that will keep you young forever?" Margot asked. The woman's unnatural question and hungry eyes made Margot shift in her chair. "There isn't anything like that. You can't cheat death," she said lightly, to end the conversation.

"Is it rare? Is that why you keep it to yourself?" The woman's voice was cold. She took a thick ring with a large clear stone from her finger and set it before Margot. "That will be yours if you tell me, Lady."

Margot didn't touch the ring. She didn't want the woman to

make the disturbing offer again. "There's nothing in the Sea that will stop you from growing old." This was the truth, unsoftened, so that the woman wouldn't mistake her meaning. "I'm sorry," she said, though she wasn't.

The woman picked up her ring. "I'll find it, Lady," she said in the same cold voice. "You won't keep it from me."

The woman left, but Margot was still uncomfortable. There would be others like her. They'd want impossible things. Or they might hunger to misuse what she told them. She should have realized this before.

More weavers in bright gowns asked about Sea plants and dyes. Fishermen who stank of brine and smoky fires wanted ways to trap the seals that chewed holes in their nets. As they asked their questions and touched her hands for luck, she was reminded of gulls demanding all she had and gobbling what she gave them. She needed to clear her head. The tall woman had made her like this.

She rose and excused herself. Meynard told her Orrin had gone to the garden, if she wanted to see him. Once out the door, she raised her face to the late-day sun. Then she stared at the Sea. She wanted to walk all over the shore and see if the light would appear. Maybe she wouldn't return to the dim hall until tomorrow.

She went to the gate at her left. A stony-faced swordsman opened it, and Margot walked past the flowers of summer's end: pale vine violets, lanky red elrosings, tiny golden lenimars. Then the flower beds ended and a garden of trees began. It was full of wood's heart and blackspine. The trunks were bent and gnarled, as were all the trees here. That was one thing she missed about the midlands—the tall straight trees.

Under the crooked branches of a wood's heart, on a stone bench, sat Orrin. "I'm glad to see you," he said. He looked tired; under his eyes were dark smudges. They sat silently. Margot didn't feel she had to speak. Her head was already clearer.

Then Orrin put his hand on the tree behind him and showed her a large hole, maybe an abandoned squirrel's nest. "When I was a boy, I used to hide things in this heart's wood. Dried toads and dead starfish. My treasures. It seemed to watch over them and make sure they stayed hidden for me."

Imagining him younger, with an angry, lonely face, Margot looked up at the boughs. They reached out like old men's arms, embracing the wind that rippled her hair. The branches reminded her of a story of a boy who tricked a huge hairy giant. A tree had moved its boughs so that the giant couldn't see him. "Maybe it did hide them for you. Like the tree in 'The Lad and the Giant.'"

Orrin leaned against the gnarled heart's wood, his face solemn. "That's a forbidden story. The lad steals gold from the giant. We don't make heroes of thieves."

Margot ran her fingernail over her arm ring's ridged tail. She'd never thought much about the stealing. She'd only noticed that the lad had tricked such a large giant. "When I was little, I liked it," she admitted.

"Why?" Orrin asked, still grave but also curious.

"He was small. And the giant was big, huge." She meant to sound calm and clever. Instead, she could hear dismay in her voice. She remembered how she'd loved this story. The smell of man-flesh in the giant's house had made the lad shiver. She had shivered, too. The boy had crouched in the house, which he'd found by accident. Then he'd sprung up. "The tree hid him, and he escaped. He made me feel as if I could escape." She hadn't known this until now, but it was true. She couldn't imagine never hearing the story again.

"He could have escaped without the gold. Small thieves are still thieves," Orrin insisted. "You won't really miss it."

"I will," she answered. Then she wished she hadn't. He knew more about this than she did; he was probably right.

"You sound like you're defending the story. Like you think me wrong to forbid it." His lips were thin. "You'd rather have that story and demon spirits than be as free as we are?"

"Of course not." She really shouldn't have said anything.

"So you do think I'm right to forbid the tale," Orrin said, giving a tight smile.

What she thought was that she didn't feel as she should. Forbidding the tale meant it was lost, gone. She hated that "The Lad and the Giant" would be gone. "I love being able to look at the stars," she told him, trying not to care about what she'd have to give up.

His smile faded, as if he'd heard the doubt in her voice. He gazed off to the side, not at her, and she felt suddenly less worthy of being looked in the eye. "You'll see, you won't really miss it."

She'd disappointed him. Why couldn't she feel what she was supposed to about the stupid story?

They were both quiet, as if neither knew what to say. She couldn't sit here. She stood and tried to see past the trees and the wall to the water. "We could walk," she suggested.

"All right," he said. He stood and offered her his arm. She took it. Her shoulder grazed against him, her hip was near his. Still, he seemed lost in his own thoughts. Maybe he was realizing she was a little less than he'd hoped. As they walked, she didn't speak; every thought that came into her head seemed disappointing. They passed the old trees and the late-summer flowers, then walked by the swordsman at the wall's gate. They went down the hillside stairs and stepped onto sand and rocks.

Wind brushed the back of Margot's neck. That, at least, felt good. She headed for the water, taking their regular route. She wished she could think of something else to do, something that would dazzle him.

"What can you see?" he asked. He sounded interested, as usual, though in the Sea, not her. "Why are you walking so close to the water?"

She wanted to have an impressive answer to offer, one that might make him forget their conversation in the garden. But all she could say was "Nothing," which was true. The light wasn't there.

Too often she walked into the water and soaked her clothing. She meant to stop now, but was unable to resist. She stepped straight into the foam, submerging her boots and drenching the edge of her gown. Rather than leaping back, Orrin walked with her. His black boots darkened as water seeped into the leather. Then, in one deft movement, he reached down and splashed her.

Her mouth dropped open. He smiled at her, one eyebrow raised in a challenge. Surprised, relieved, she hesitated a moment, then reached down and tried to splash him. He moved too quickly. She tried again, but he escaped. She drew back her leg and kicked. Water flew out before her in a huge, satisfying spray. His hair and his long overtunic were soaked. He shook himself like a dog and laughed.

Laughter burst out of Margot, too. His silver circlet was askew and strands of his hair were straggling around his face. Out here, she wasn't disappointing, and he didn't seem to care if she ever had been. "We could walk in the water," she said, only half teasing. She meandered out farther. "Why stay on the land when we're already wet?"

"True enough," he said, laughing again. "But you must have

thick skin. The wind is blowing straight through me. I need dry clothes."

"I'm coming," said Margot, although she didn't start forward. The wide, wide water was so blue and swirling. It tugged at her knees. She wanted, even if just for one moment, to be in it. In it, within it, entirely surrounded. She turned and plunged in.

The land disappeared; there was only water. Everything—her fingernails, her eyelids, the ends of her hair—felt the endless sway and swell all around her. Her eyes stung from the salt, but she kept them open. Colors blurred and shifted as she watched them, first growing more blue, then more gray, then more green, shifting and shifting and shifting again. Her dress tangled around her. She kicked hard, swimming into the Sea's cold and strength.

Fish flickered ahead of her, heading toward a deeper darkness. She followed them, though she needed to lift her head and breathe. Then she realized the lead fish wasn't a fish at all. It was a flickering light. Its brilliance reached out in all directions, like the light in her book.

She tried to swim to it, but it floated ahead of her, leading her somewhere. She kicked harder, reaching toward the brightness. Her dress dragged at her. Her lungs ached.

The light continued into the dark, too fast for her to keep up. She craved air. Then the water's darkness swallowed it. She blew out her stale breath as she swam toward the surface.

"Margot!" Orrin was up to his knees in water. He was leaning over, as if he'd been trying to see her through the waves. "Where were you going? Did you see something?"

"There's a light out there. In the water." She pointed. Then she dived back down.

# Fourteen

argot sat in her draelan guesthouse, on the bed's
stiff pallet. The previous day, when she had dived
back into the Sea, she hadn't found the light.
She'd looked until late. Orrin had looked. He'd
called other holy men to help. They hadn't seen a glimpse. She
stared down at her book in her lap, and at the map. All the lines
had a blue-silver shine. The Sea's swells and troughs rippled
across the page. The light glowed under the water. It brightened and faded, brightened and faded and brightened. So it
would appear again in the water. It would.

She felt slow-witted. Her mother and the other women had
understood the map and the book. She didn't. She shut it. She
stared at the cover. Then she licked the leather. It tasted like
Sea water, but knowing the cover's taste didn't help her understand the book.

She'd go look for the light again. She put the book in her
sack, then tucked it under blankets in a trunk. She went out,
stepped over the draelan wall, and found the holy men's path
to the Sea. Despite the sun, the damp air was chilly. She should
have brought a cloak but didn't go back. She followed the curving path. Partway down, she halted.

She could see the shore below. Gray-robed holy men walked or stood talking. Some were also in a small boat. They were rowing for Orrin. His light hair shone in a way that made her want to touch it. He was bent over, and the hand trailing in the water also shone. He had learned, Meynard had explained proudly, to send his magic forward, and he could feel the shape of whatever the magic touched. This was hard to do. He'd exhausted himself the day before and had needed help to get to his room. She'd also left the Sea so that she could sleep, but it looked as though the holy men had stayed up all night: a few tall torches still burned at the water's edge.

She didn't go down. The holy men stood or walked along the shore. Two slogged in the water, pulling another boat. Altogether, ten to fifteen men were there, more than the day before. It wasn't her shore, her Sea, or her light, but they hadn't asked her to stay up all night with them. They hadn't woken her, or come to find out when she'd join them. They'd arranged the search as if she weren't part of it.

If they'd found the light, would they have come and told her? Would they tell her what it was, or say she didn't need to know because it was magic and she was a girl? She traced the ring on her upper arm, watching the boat and Orrin. Would he tell her?

The question didn't drift away.

She traced the arm ring again, feeling the powerful tail and the proud head.

He'd tell her they'd found it, but he wouldn't explain if he thought he shouldn't. Suddenly, intensely, she wanted Belinde. Belinde would say, with a smile, that this shouldn't upset her. She should just convince Orrin.

Margot didn't find the idea of convincing him as comfortable as she knew Belinde would. She wished he understood without having to be convinced.

Orrin straightened, the glow in his hands dying away. The holy men began to row him in. He caught sight of her and waved. The wave was so broad and eager, it made her worries lessen a little. She waved back.

She met the holy men on the rocky shore. Orrin kissed her hand and smiled, looking both worn out and exhilarated. "We'd like to ask you about the light again," he said.

*Not now,* Margot almost replied. She wanted to talk with him alone, not answer questions. "Maybe after we're done searching today?" she asked.

He touched her arm. "But it might help our search this morning," he said as Meynard and two older holy men came over.

Margot glanced at them. They stood around Orrin, their faces also tired but excited. She supposed she wasn't part of "our search"; he meant his and theirs. She tried not to care.

"All right, I'll talk with them," she said, just wanting it over and done with.

"What color was the light?" Meynard asked, half glancing at the water. "Was it deep in the water?"

"White," she answered. She'd already told him this. "Somewhat deep."

"Did it look like a creature?" he asked, speaking quickly.

She shook her head with impatience; she'd told him this before, as well. "No."

His next question cut off her answer. "What did it look like?"

"A star, almost," she replied.

"With no other shape?" Meynard went on.

"No." They asked questions. She answered. It was as if she were a trained hound. *Sit. Stay. Walk.* Orrin didn't object or even seem to notice. She could feel a too sharp response right behind her teeth. "And I didn't see it for long," she said; she'd be helpful instead.

"There must be something more," Meynard told the others, consulting them, not her.

"What do you think it is?" she asked, some sharpness coming out, although she hadn't meant it to.

Orrin flushed; she seemed to have embarrassed him. The others looked disapproving. "We can't explain magics to you." Meynard spoke as if he were instructing a child. "And it must be a kind of magic. Though if it's one the demon spirits might use or one we might use against them, we don't know."

"We can't tell you more," Orrin added, no longer smiling. "You know that." Still flushed, he looked to the holy men rather than at her.

"I saw the light. It appeared to *me*," she snapped, then wished she hadn't. Orrin's expression had gone grim and angry. He was in the wrong, but she'd never convince him this way.

"You have water in your blood. You know and see things. But you can't think you should work magic." Orrin gave a false smile, just a showing of teeth. The others laughed at her for thinking such a thing, and maybe at him, too, for having to remind her that she shouldn't.

"Surely not." She spoke flatly. The holy men finished laughing and Meynard nodded with approval. Orrin stayed as he was. His smile was still false. He knew she didn't really mean what she said.

"How did the light move?" asked Meynard. "Tell us all you can."

She looked at Meynard and the two balding old men beside him. They'd keep demanding, then examine everything she knew of water. They'd decide what they thought about it without any say from her. Orrin stood with them. For now, he'd do the same. Walking away wouldn't make him understand, but at this moment, she didn't want to be near any of them. "My head hurts," she told them. "Excuse me."

⌒⊙⌒

She walked fast among the rocks and boulders, half lost in the paths. The longer she walked, the worse she felt. She hadn't deftly won Orrin over, she'd embarrassed and angered him. He wouldn't sit down beside her. He wouldn't lean toward her and talk about anything and everything. Not right now.

She'd been so stupid. But it wasn't entirely her fault. In Pristanne, she'd been tainted. Here, she was useful. Useful could be important; it was important. Cooking pots, though, were also useful, as were trained hounds and many other things that were meant to serve or obey. She didn't even want to go near the feast hall. People would be waiting to ask her for answers. They might think her more important than a cooking pot, but she no longer wanted to be useful at the moment. And she didn't know how to say all this so that Orrin would understand.

Margot walked until her hands were chilled. She thought of going to him. She just wanted to say the perfect words. Then she might step near to him as she sometimes did, briefly, so no one would whisper too much about them. Their hands would be close. His thumb would run down the side of hers. Or his palm would cup the back of her hand, his larger fingers cradling her smaller ones.

She was scared that, instead, she wouldn't explain in the right way. She'd make him angrier. Not only would he not touch her, he wouldn't *want* to touch her. So she headed back to her guesthouse rather than to the castle. Avoiding the gate, she climbed over the draelan wall. She crept to her house. She listened at the door. He might have started looking for her. She

*117*

hoped he hadn't. She wasn't ready to see him. She needed to figure out how to be like Belinde, charming and able to set everything right.

She heard only silence, so she opened the door. Orrin stood by the hearth. Her riding gowns and an undergown were on the floor. Her second pair of boots lay on top of them. Blankets had been torn off the pallet. His face was livid, and he held a book with a worn green cover. It looked old, ancient. Margot felt as if her insides were sinking to her feet. It was *The Book of the Sea.* "Give that to me, Orrin," she said.

"I could tell that you knew more than you were saying. I thought maybe you'd picked up something that you didn't want to talk about. So I came to look. This book smells of deep magic, and it tried to hide from me. I had to use strong spells to find it," he said bitterly. His voice held pain, raw hurt, which she'd caused. "You couldn't have just come across this. You've been lying all these months. You should have told me. When we first met, you should have told me."

She felt as though he had thrust her before an unfamiliar mirror. Her reflection showed a liar, a cruel one. That was not her, not wholly, but a piece of it was. She had left Pristanne knowing she wouldn't tell him about her book. Her secret had seemed small then, but it didn't anymore. She wanted to wipe away the cruel, deceitful reflection and make that piece of her disappear.

"You have to tell me," he insisted. "And you can't shame me or yourself by demanding to know more about magic that isn't yours to understand."

Her anger rushed up. "What if I demanded you tell me about holy man magics?" Margot said. "Not asked or requested, demanded? What if I made you tell me everything I asked?"

His face went paler than she'd ever seen it. "Do you really

mean to compare the two: water in the blood and being a holy man? I have reasons, judgment, training, which all require I keep the draelan's secrets."

"But I can't have reasons or judgment. I take commands and obey. If I want to have a say about this book or about what I know, I'm shameful and hateful. That's what you're telling me." She wouldn't cry. "The book doesn't hide from *me*. It never has. It only hides from other people. People it doesn't belong to."

"You're so ignorant. You don't know anything about magic. You can't just decide to do things your own way." Orrin grabbed Margot's arm. "What is this book? Its words are all faded, but one of them clearly says Sea. Yet inside it's empty." He held it lower so she could study it, astonished. The cover was more faded and brown than before. The title, *The Book of the Sea*, was almost unreadable. The inside pages held nothing. It had transformed itself again, Margot realized with bleak satisfaction. The book could lock Orrin out. "Where did you steal this from?" he asked.

Margot reached for it. "It's mine, from my mother. It belongs to me," she told him, though he wouldn't agree. She no longer knew how she'd ever thought he would.

"Belongs to you." He spat out the words. "Your mother was wrong to have it, and so are you. You really can't see that, can you? It must be a magic thing from the Sea. Holy men should've had this long ago. We could've already known more Sea magics. We could be using them."

She pulled her arm free. "What I know isn't just useful to you," she said. Had he only wanted to learn what she knew? Was that all he'd ever liked about her? "You're the one stealing from me."

"You accuse me?" he asked. To him, she was all wrong and

he was all right. But this wasn't a forbidden story or something else he knew more about; this was her book. "You're the liar. You knew all my draelan and I are trying to learn everything we can about the Sea's secrets. You knew the book was magic. Yet you didn't hand it over to me."

"How could I have told you?" Margot was shaking with fury and humiliation; he wasn't really listening to her. "You want to take it away."

"You'll be locked in until you tell me how this book works," he said, disregarding her reply. "I know better than to trust you. There will always be a swordsman at the door. If you do tell me, you might go free someday. Lady. This is your chance to right yourself," he said; then he left.

"My book!" Margot yelled after him. "I don't want your chances, I want my book. Bring it back!"

Her mother's writing and the names on the first page. The smell of Sea, the map, the pages that had once held pictures. All gone.

And the door was shut—he'd locked her in.

This was not home. He no longer loved her, maybe he never really had. She'd once seen a house fall in. The walls had shifted and collapsed. The roof had plunged down, its wood splintering. A loud cracking noise had sounded all around. She felt as if that house were falling inside her.

# Fifteen

ird opened his eyes. The innkeep stood over him. She was as broad as a man, and carried a cudgel. The old nursescrub rhyme sounded in his head: *Jack Sprat could eat no fat, his wife could eat no lean.*

She nudged him with her boot and whispered, "Get out." Bird began to nod, then stopped. He'd drunk too much last night; he felt as if a sharp spike had been nailed into his forehead. He should have known he'd gone too far when he accepted the inn specialty—sour wine mixed with old goat's milk and fat, sprinkled with something they simply called "spice."

As the innkeep kicked one of the floor pallets other men were lying on, Bird heard footsteps thudding down the hall. "Swordsmen are raiding. If any of you have forbidden or stolen goods, you'd better take them with you. I won't be dragged to prison because of you trash," the innkeep whispered to the men pushing themselves up; then she disappeared out the door.

Bird stood, his stomach clenching as he noticed the stink of spilled beer, piss, and vomit. The innkeep could make a new specialty from the floor scrapings; she probably would. He followed a grimy boatman across the crowded, dirty room. Other men rose, agile, though they'd drunk more than he had. The boatman shoved open the shutters and climbed out the window into the dawn. From listening to them last night, he knew they were used to swordsmen appearing and grabbing people from Portside. He also knew that being grabbed, even if one had done nothing wrong, meant prison. Few were able to convince the swordsmen to release them.

Bird followed, slow and clumsy. Not only did he not want to go to prison, he'd be ashamed if he was captured: a bunch of men, some of them twice his age and still full of sour wine and old goat's milk, had outrun him already. He had to move faster.

Once on the muddy ground, he dashed around the edge of the inn. He didn't look back to see if the other men had been caught, just as they wouldn't look after him. The sun was rising, but the maze of Portside streets was dark because the buildings were so close together. He went around a few more corners. Some scrawny chickens roosting on window ledges startled, and scolded him. Besides them, he was alone. He slowed. The swordsmen must have stayed at the inn and grabbed whom they could. Maybe someday he'd know the names of those taken. He now meant to return to Portside as often as he could. Coming here had given him the kind of heady rush he felt when he tumbled hand over foot, spinning like a cart's wheel, the way a jester had taught him to.

The night before, he'd seen someone show off a knife made with forbidden spells. A woman had sold her body for food. Yet he'd also heard things people elsewhere seemed never to say. A boatmen had told of honest trade lost because of Orrin's travel restrictions. The innkeep had complained that swordsmen walking the roads demanded free meals from those who had little to spare. A boy had jested about a holy man braggart who hadn't looked where he was stepping and had ended up in the sewer. They hadn't endlessly praised Beloved Orrin, either. They hadn't said his every victory was glorious. They hadn't spoken of his triumphs as always perfect, never marred by mistakes or flaws. They thought as Bird did.

As he'd listened, Bird had also felt, for the first time in a long while, a kind of aching hope. Here, someone might ask him for a forbidden story. The kind in which good wasn't all good and bad wasn't all bad. Orrin claimed such tales caused criminals to be. Bird didn't agree. They told about how people really were. Not telling or hearing them seemed like a lie. The same way, Bird realized, saying that Orrin's victories were all perfect seemed like a lie.

And Bird missed those stories. He tried not to think about them, but they were always there, inside him. He'd found watching a woman sell herself and hearing a thief brag about his knife disturbing. Still, it had been so long since he'd told a story in which the hero was foolish, uncertain, or mean, more like a real man. He wanted to be asked for one, and to speak it aloud. More than anything. He probably wouldn't mind that Beloved Orrin bragged and had to be always in the right, never in the wrong—he probably wouldn't care at all if he could just tell and hear the stories he loved.

He had to return to the draelan guesthouse where his father slept, but he took a meandering route. Ragged women came out with full buckets to dump in the ditches. Fishermen walked home with their early-morning strings of fish. A cooper rolled a cask down the street. Bird wondered if the cask would go to Elene, once the weaver's daughter, now wife to a brewer's son. He had never meant to marry her, but he still missed her the way he missed sunshine in the stormy months. In a way, she hadn't just told him she wouldn't meet him in the dye house anymore, then wed someone else. She'd locked away the woman he'd secretly known in the dark; *that* woman would never have married a man she thought boring and clumsy.

He turned onto the bigger road. Then he crossed it and started over the bracken and rocks. As he headed up the hill toward the castle, his stomach tightened again. He'd have to slip on his impassive mask. He wanted, instead, to tell a tale of a fool king tricked by a peasant. In the illusion he longed to weave, the king would resemble Orrin.

He glanced up at the tall castle, gray stone against a gray sky. The Lady was the one brightness in it right now. Watching her would be worth wearing a mask. Bird hadn't expected to like her and he didn't think she liked him much, but she had a good laugh. She'd also spoken her request the night before and had released Gwist's name, his memory, on Orrin's feast hall. She wasn't defiant, just ignorant. Still, Bird looked forward to seeing what else she might do.

At the top of the hill, he swerved. Instead of going over the low draelan wall, he headed toward the cliff face and the rocks. He perched on a boulder and looked out at the Sea. The water's pounding made his head worse, and he had to go inside to his father. But he didn't move. He began to whisper the words to the tale the Lady had asked for. He closed his eyes and savored the sound of the story, though he was the only one to hear.

A voice called, "Bird."

Breaking off, Bird stood and saw his father leaning heavily on a walking stick as he made his way through the rocks. The storyteller's face was sallow. Bird leapt down. He should have returned to the draelan earlier. "Are you feeling worse? You shouldn't have come up here," he said. Bird had thought his father was easily improving this time. He'd have to stop wandering until the illness subsided again. The thought made his limbs heavier. "Someone else would have fetched me."

"Well, I had to find you first. I told you the other day that the king keeps asking where you go," said the storyteller sharply. "You have to try harder to be there when he calls for you."

Bird smiled at the scolding; his father couldn't be that ill. "He doesn't like hearing me," Bird said. "Only you."

"Still. When he wants you, he wants you. That's how it is." The storyteller looked out at the Sea and the sky. He seemed to listen, as Bird did, to the cries of gulls and the crashing of waves. "You need to stop going to Portside, or wherever you go," the storyteller said. "Do you want to be judged disgraced and forced to wear an iron band around your neck? If you break the king's laws, if he judges you disgraced, I can't pass the stories and magic of our storytelling line to you. I'll have to search out a new apprentice or all our tales will go to the spirit realms with me when I die. They'll leave these lands forever." His father gestured at him with the round-headed walking stick. "Is that what you want?"

"I don't want them to die," Bird said. He tried not to sound so angry. "I want all our stories to be heard."

"So you'll be a criminal and only tell tales for criminals? You've considered that?" His father's tone was biting but also amused. "You'd hate to watch them steal and kill. You'd hate it as much as telling pallid stories to Orrin. You need to learn to like what your king asks for or you might as well cut out your tongue.

"Orrin's laws might go too far, but most think that his forbidding stories has helped keep us safe, and maybe it has."

"Do stories really make more criminals? We don't know. Orrin doesn't know. He didn't try to find out. He just wanted the tales gone," Bird said. He'd thought this before but had never said it aloud. He hadn't been sure it was true. Hearing it in the air, he was.

"Maybe." The storyteller let out a long sigh. Then he stared steadily at Bird. "I can't find another apprentice. My time is almost gone. Frankly, I thought it might run out as I searched for you."

Bird stared back at him, noticing for the first time the ravages of the illness. His skin was parchment thin. His eyes burned too brightly. He'd clamped his hands on his walking stick, his knuckles pale from holding too tightly to the last remnants of life.

"Swear you'll stop going to Portside," said his father. "If you keep Mawr's king, holy men, and lords happy, at least all the stories will be alive within you. Things change. You may be able to tell them again, or those to whom you'll pass the line will. You have to swear, though." The storyteller's face grew fiercer. "I could take the stories with me. The line might as well end with me if you're going to end it anyway."

Bird didn't argue this time. He didn't move. Stories no one heard weren't alive, but his father deserved to be free of worries. He was heading toward death's gatekeeper. He wouldn't be coming back.

A piece of Bird demanded: *Don't leave me.* He couldn't say that; he wasn't a boy. "I won't let the line die. I swear," he said, meeting his father's too bright stare.

"And you'll stop going to Portside," his father insisted.

Bird had to give his father ease, even if it meant speaking an oath he'd break. "I swear."

They kept staring at each other, silent. The Sea and gulls were making noise, but far away, as if outside a thin wall. Bird wanted to inherit his father's magic, his stories, and the right to weave new tales. He wanted to find out how magic passed and become a master storyteller. He wanted to turn and run. Once his father passed on the magic, he'd no longer be Tomos Silvertongue. He'd be only a sick man waiting to die.

The storyteller reached out. His hand clasped Bird's. Instead of the wasted fingers, Bird felt a burning heat. It was like fire spreading into his throat and heart and belly. Sweat dripped down his face.

The burning went through him. He had no arms and no eyes. There was no god or demon; there were no spirits, no men, no women, no lands. There was him that was heat, and heat that was him.

Burning. Burning. Burning.

Then it was gone.

Bird crouched, and his father let go of him. His palms felt raw. They were blistered and tender. They had a new line, which crossed the fate, love, and life lines. It was the one that only the master storyteller had, the line of the tales. It hurt.

And his head hurt. It was full of words. They sailed through him like wild, wheeling hawks. He could never tame them all.

His father smiled, but his shoulders drooped. His face looked so old now it seemed young, like that of a newborn babe. He'd dropped his walking stick. His hands hung open, empty. They no longer clutched desperately at life. "You'll do well."

Bird nodded. He felt lost, and he couldn't stop looking at his father's hands. Open hands, holding nothing.

# Sixteen

ird's back ached. His palms were blistered. He piled the stones on his father's grave. Then he put his head against the stones.

He'd been up all night, sitting with his father's body. The holy men had brought a cask of wine and candles. A handful of men and women, the best storytellers and minstrels from the city, had come to sit. They'd told tales, sung, and drunk. They'd helped him clean and wrap the body. At dawn, the holy men had carried it to this valley burial ground and said their rites. Then Bird had told them to go. It had taken him all day to dig, then fill, the grave himself. Now it was done.

Bird sat back on his heels, looking over the older rock mounds. He couldn't stop seeing his father's hands. They had been larger than his. Even after passing on the magic, his father had used them when he talked. He'd gestured in the air. He'd touched Bird's fingers lightly as he'd asked for stories. He'd wanted all his favorites, as long as they weren't ones Orrin had forbidden. After Bird told each one, his father had said, *Keep telling them, keep telling them,* though he'd been too tired to listen and had stood in the doorway of his own death. Bird had spoken them, even after he'd realized he was alone in the room: the hands were still and his father had finally gone.

Bird bent down again. He pressed his forehead hard against the stones, but it still didn't hurt as much as he did inside.

After a long while, Bird straightened and pushed himself up. Orrin would expect him soon. He began to walk beside the tall wall that encircled Syllig and the castle. Then he took a turn that led to the city instead of up the castle's hill. He couldn't be near Orrin and those who praised him today. He didn't even care to see the Lady. It was time to break the oath he'd made to his father: he wanted the stench of Portside.

He turned onto the muddy road and passed a great house. Men were stacking piles of peat and dried manure for winter fires. The cold, blowing storms weren't far away. Now that Bird was no longer Tomos Silvertongue's apprentice, Orrin might tell him to leave. He had nowhere to go. His mother lived too far in the mountains to reach before winter. Besides, she preferred her own company; although married, she and his father had never lived together. She was glad to see them once a year or so, and glad when they left her. He traced the red feathers he'd sewn all around the edge of his cloak the night before. It was late to find a new place to winter. Even if he did, little would be different. All of Mawr obeyed Orrin. Throughout the westlands, the draelans followed Mawr's draelans. The holy men trained spirit hunters and advised lords and kings to forbid stories, restrict travel, train more swordsmen. It had started to seem as if Orrin was the king of holy men, Bird had heard. He began to walk more quickly.

He took the curving street toward the docks, where the long low boats would be tied. The street grew narrower. The men and women on it wore rougher clothes, and ragged dogs scavenged. Then the shadows, the beggar children, and the sharp smell of a clogged sewer made him slow. If he went past the next building, with the shutterless holes for windows, he'd be in Portside. He rubbed the back of one hand where his father had touched him and asked for the last stories. His forehead hurt where he'd pressed it against the grave stones.

He felt heavy, dragged down. He'd never meant to keep the oath, but he couldn't break it today. He turned around.

A cutting wind began to blow. He wandered as the sky grew dark. Down a broader street, ahead of him, was a slightly battered sign. The word INN was painted on it, as well as a boat. The boat's flag was red and gold. It rested in a calm harbor. He wanted the calm harbor the sign promised, just for one night.

Once through the heavy door, he found a dark, warm, smoke-filled eating hall. It wasn't a large hall, just a room the right size for twenty or so to sit in, and wasn't full. Several men glanced over at him from their seats near the fire. Then they went back to their tankards and trenchers. A short woman with silver-white hair piled high and pinned tightly met him by the door. "You have coppers?"

He pulled the coins out of his almost empty purse and gave the innkeep enough for one night and a supper. She looked hard at them. Then she hid them away so fast he wasn't sure where she'd put them. "I expect the room to be left the way you find it, nothing broken or missing. The window is barred, so don't plan to climb out with my blankets or candle. Supper is served down here. I don't bring food to rooms. If you do anything I don't like, you leave without your coins. Is that all clear?"

He smiled slightly. "Perfectly, Innkeep."

"Sharp Maud. That's what everyone calls me."

He studied her. He was surprised she kept the name, since stories of Sharp Maud were now forbidden. Sharp Maud had been a pirate who'd harried the boats of westlander kings a few hundred years back. She'd ruled her crew with ferocity and a roguish honor.

Sharp Maud gestured to his black cloak and its edging of red marnloy feathers. "Maybe you'll tell us a tale, storyteller. A decent tale." The way she'd said "decent" caught at Bird. She'd stressed it, as if she hadn't heard a decent tale in a long while and was challenging him to tell one. Then he almost laughed. She couldn't be. This wasn't Portside.

The laughter faded away. He thought of all the wretched tales she might call for. She might even ask if he had one that would praise Orrin. The night loomed before him. "If I know one you'd like," he answered, wearing his mask of polite interest.

"Maybe you don't. I'm particular about the stories I have told under my roof." She sounded contemptuous. She began walking in the other direction, up a set of stairs. She stopped when she noticed he wasn't following. "Are you coming or not?"

Had she been daring him? Had she wished him to tell a forbidden tale? That couldn't be what she'd wished. He wanted her to, that was all.

"Well?" Her stern face gave none of her thoughts away.

"I'm coming," he answered, trying to crush out the flare of want. It blazed, tenacious.

She led him to a small room with a sloping but well-scrubbed floor and an angled ceiling. As he set his sack down, she said, "You'd better come eat soon or the food will be gone. I don't serve beer or wine to men who won't put something else in their guts first." She sounded as if she was done with him, but she didn't leave. She crossed her arms. Her head tilted slightly to one side. She seemed to be waiting for him to tell her something.

The want flared higher. "And that's all?" he asked.

"It is," she answered in her contemptuous way, and swept out, leaving him alone.

His want, his hope that she'd ask, was gone as quickly as it had come. He felt colder than before, and emptier. He threw his sack on the bed. In the morning he'd go to Portside. He'd find people who wanted to hear what he wanted to tell. His father was mistaken; to keep forbidden tales from dying, he could share a table with any kind of fool or criminal.

He sat on the floor, his back against the bed frame. Words still wheeled in him sometimes, as they had right after he'd inherited the magic. Tonight they all seemed to be about death: *Beneath. Swan. Frigid. Lakewood. Drowned.* He'd ask his father how to weave them together. Maybe he'd make a new tale Orrin would forbid. Then, with a start, he remembered he'd never speak to his father again. His eyes hurt. He began to rock. He rocked, and tearless sobs heaved through him.

He went down late. He wasn't hungry but couldn't sleep. The words had gone silent. The sobs had stopped. He felt hollow.

He took a seat at the long table closest to the smoky fire. A serving maid brought him a tankard of bitter ale and all that was left to eat, a weak eel stew. As Bird hunched over his bowl, a man beside him said, "So. You're a storyteller."

Bird set his spoon down. If he'd been thinking more clearly, he'd have pulled magic into his hands and released an illusion of grayness around himself. He'd have made his cloak and face drab. Then no one would have noticed him. He didn't want to have to smile and tell a tale he hated. "I am," he answered.

"Storyteller. Or bootlicker. That's what we should call them," the man went on. He swayed a bit. "Used to be storytellers were men. They didn't tell all these bootlicking tales."

The clanks and talking stopped. Bird thought he must have misheard. He leaned on one arm, closer to the man. "What do you mean?"

A woman's voice, tight and too high, said, "Shut your mouth, Kiernan One-Arm. The king's made it safe for you to drink at night and walk home with your friends. You should be happy."

A few laughed, glancing at the door for swordsmen or at the room's shadows, as if such talk could draw demon spirits. Kiernan ignored them. "I mean," Kiernan said to Bird, "the good stories tell about this good king and that good holy man, and everyone's in his right place doing his right thing. A man doesn't always feel that way, does he? Does he?"

"If a man doesn't always feel that way," the woman called angrily to Kiernan, "he should. Now stop."

Bird stared at mule-faced Kiernan. He must have made the one-armed man out of hope and words: this was illusion, not real.

The click and then the bang of a door opening and shutting startled Bird. Beside him, Kiernan jumped. It was the kitchen door, though, not the one to the street. Sharp Maud leaned against the frame. She surveyed the eating hall. Her look stopped on Bird. "You'll have the king's swordsmen coming in my place, Kiernan," she said, still looking at Bird. Her tone threatened, or dared him.

Bird could hear the kind of answer, the kind of story Kiernan wanted murmuring deep inside him. It echoed inside all the vast empty spaces. Sharp Maud was playing some game. In the last year, no one had asked him for a forbidden tale. No one, not even during the other night in Portside. She couldn't truly be asking, either. This was not a safe game to play.

"As if the swordsmen or demon spirits scare you, Sharp Maud," Kiernan answered. "You're more a man than anyone in this room."

"I'm particular about the tales told under my roof," Sharp Maud said. To Bird, it seemed she was speaking just to him. "I only want the best."

Bird had trouble finding his voice. "Do you?"

"The best," she repeated, coming over to him. She stood behind him so that he had to rise and turn to face her. Then she whispered, "Like one about Sharp Maud."

The whisper shuddered through Bird. The murmuring sea of story rose. The story swelled to a thundering rush, dragging magic out of his bones. He raised his hands. Magic poured from them down his forearms. It filled all the emptiness.

> *"Beneath the waves, in a place made of stone and darkness, lives the seal woman."*

Story and magic twined around each other, twined around him. He made the words and the words made him.

He was the seal woman, full of savage sorrow and fury after a westlander king hunted and killed her mate. She left her palace and sought out Sharp Maud, the first Sharp Maud, with hair cut short and dagger eyes. Near the pirate ship, the seal pulled off her skin and flung it around her like a cape. Then she climbed the ship's side.

> *"You'll never meet your death on the Sea, Sharp Maud,*
> *if you do this one thing for me:*
> *Chase the westlander king's boat.*
> *Harry it.*
> *Show it no mercy.*

*My storm won't touch you,*
*but it'll tear that boat's sails and*
*break its boards and*
*swallow its crew whole."*

The seal woman cut herself. She dripped blood into the Sea, which raised a storm. Sharp Maud found the king's boat. She attacked it, driving it into the howling, raving gale. The storm roared; the westlanders' boat broke to pieces; Sharp Maud laughed with ruthless triumph. The storm swallowed the men. Sealskins drifted to the Sea floor.

The seal woman came for her mate's skin. She cradled the skin as if her mate still wore it. She laid it down, smoothing and kissing it. Then she left it.

*"And so the seal woman returned to the place made of stone*
*and darkness.*
*Alone, she returned.*
*And alone she is still."*

The story hovered in silence.

Someone touched the silence. No, not the silence—him. Someone touched him.

He shifted. He was not the skin, or the seal woman, or Sharp Maud. He was not words and story.

He was Bird.

"Walk with me. You need to leave here before the dazzle wears off them. Several will run to tell the king's swordsmen." Fingers pinched his arm hard. They were a woman's fingers, Sharp Maud's.

He was not in the Sea. He was in the inn's smoky eating hall. Men and women, with forgotten tankards before them, stared at him. There were tears. Not on every face, but on some. And a satisfaction with revenge. He began to shake. They weren't thieves and killers, but they felt all this for a forbidden story, as he did.

Sharp Maud led him through a door into a dark hallway. "You're shuddering like these walls in a high wind. Don't tell me you're ill."

"I'm fine." He halted. She was Sharp Maud the innkeep, not Sharp Maud of the stories. She could turn him in. "This doesn't lead to the street."

"You can't go out the front. There's more chance of someone recognizing you." Sharp Maud pulled on his arm. "I'm taking you to the back door. I'll say it was another storyteller, Guy the Northman, who used to winter with that lord of the marshlands, Lord Neil. He recently told forbidden tales and fled. He looks much like you, and if I say that's who came into my place, no one will doubt it. Do as you usually do, and you'll be safe enough."

She started again. He followed, still shaking, his thoughts hard to catch hold of. He hadn't heard about Guy the Northman. This woman had asked him to tell a forbidden story in a public inn. She'd whispered so that no one had heard her ask but him. "What happened to Guy? Why did you ask me for that tale?"

"I'm going to show you where you can find friends, a few storytellers and minstrels who want to keep alive forbidden tales and songs. They meet, in secret. They'll tell you about the Northman. And how can you ask why? Now you don't look like you might fall in the sewer ditch and not get up anymore. Isn't that reason enough? Or how about this: a pirate can sometimes have honor, a holy man can sometimes be a fool. Our king can say otherwise, but that won't make it so. Do we even know what's made the demon spirits fewer? The travel rules, the demon spirit hunters, the stories and songs that are forbidden, some reason of their own? No. I think Orrin grabs too much by telling us what we can and can't hear, what we can and can't like." She laughed a laugh that sounded both wicked and joyful. "Do you need another reason? I love a good story, and I don't get to hear one often."

Bird was sure she also loved danger. He knew better than to trust her. But he liked her.

The hallway ended with another door that was actually a pantry's false wall. They stepped into the long, wide pantry. To the side of one shelf was a panel. Sharp Maud pulled on it. It was an opening to an alley. "Come back in the middle of the week if you can. See that door, the one across the alley that looks like it's boarded shut? Knock on the boards. Mention my name."

"How do I know you aren't sending me to a swordsman's trap?" He didn't really believe she was, but he wanted to hear what she'd say.

"Think what you want. I don't have time to stand around arguing." She gave him a smile as wicked and joyful as her laugh. "It was a fine tale. A beautiful telling of a fine tale. I won't soon forget it."

A fine tale. Bird grinned; he felt he could walk on his hands all the way through the city. It was a fine tale. He bowed low to Sharp Maud, lower than he'd ever bowed to Orrin. Her smile broadened as she slammed the panel closed.

# Seventeen

rrin had left. Margot had heard him somehow lock the latch on the other side of the door. Above her, letting in moonlight and Sea air, was a window that hinged open. It was too small to climb through. She'd checked.

She stared past the fire, at the large ragged chip in one of the hearthstones. Orrin had locked her in. He had final say over her. She had *given* him say by putting herself under his protection. But she hadn't expected he'd imprison her, the way a tyrant lord shut up all who disagreed with him. She also hadn't expected him to think that what she knew belonged to him, that he was entitled to grab it if he could. He'd stolen the book. That hurt, but he was a holy man and the book was a magic thing. His intention to take, by force, her thoughts and secrets hurt her more.

Her skin felt too tight. Orrin also knew all her humiliations in Pristanne. He knew her mouth, her lips and tongue. They might have bored him or made him laugh behind her back. Even if they hadn't, she hated how much he knew of her. She pulled off the arm ring he'd given her and threw it across the room.

It landed by the hearth. It was upside down, the fish head against the floor stones, the tail in the air. She was so furious, but she also felt like crying. Why couldn't the ring be on her arm? Why couldn't they go back, to how they were before? Then, before, he'd sometimes kissed her in odd places, behind her ear, between her index finger and thumb, and once, laughing, on her elbow. She'd thought this was because he'd loved every bit of her. He might have.

What was wrong with her? She was here, now, not before, locked in this room because he was trying to take what she didn't want to give. How could she want him and "before" so badly? It was stupid and mortifying.

On the table sat a dish of water a swordsman had brought so she could wash up. Margot went to it and splashed her face. Then she let the silky drops glide off her eyelashes and down her nose. She watched them fall back into the dish. The water grew tranquil. Her reflected face was blended with moonlight and shadows. The water made her look like someone else, someone strong and fast who could escape without coins or anyone's help. She had to be that someone.

She'd have to be calm, too, like the water in the dish. She reached out and touched the clear, placid surface with her fingers. It rippled, then smoothed into stillness. She tried to take the stillness and calm inside her, to let it flow up through her fingertips.

She closed her eyes and felt the slight tension where air ended and water began. As she stood motionless, hand to water, the tension seemed to run up her arm. It was as though her skin had become the water's skin; her body, the water's body. She was liquid and light and cool.

She started to draw back her hand. Then she went motionless again. Her hand was above the water, but her skin was still interwoven with tension. She could also feel, at the end of each finger, a clinging touch. She bent so she could see her fingertips. Extending from each was a slender strand of water. The sight of them gave her a pricking feeling between her shoulder blades.

She wasn't a holy man or a storyteller, but the water's magic had reached out for her hand. It had clung to her. Or she had magic inside her, separate from her book; she had water in her blood. She stared at the strands. A small, clear voice within her suggested she try to make them go where she willed. She lifted her hand.

The water followed, rising smoothly. She could feel the strands' weight now. It was like the weight of sturdy rope but wasn't too heavy for her. She stretched her arm above her head. The water stretched above her, too. Her hand had guided it so high.

A breeze blew in from the small window. It shook the threads of water and made them sway. Margot swayed, too. As she did, a light smaller than a torchfly darted in with the wind. It was white and flickering. It was the light from the Sea, her light.

It swelled and flew straight to her hand. It perched on her thumb, grabbing with tiny talons. Suddenly, it was shaped all of feathers—not a bird, just many feathers. A voice like water shifting against sand whispered, "I felt your magic from the water. Clever, to learn this so quickly."

Wind spun through the room, more than could possibly have come through the small window opening. The tension in her skin wavered and weakened. "Who are you?" she asked, as if its voice and shape didn't disconcert her.

The wind blew. The strands swayed. The creature's gripping talons hurt. "I had to come see for myself. Your hands are stronger and steadier than I expected" was all it said.

A great gust came up, shoving her. She staggered. The tension ran out of her skin. The water fell with a splash. Much of it landed in the dish, but some also wet the table and the floor. Her arms and legs became heavy. Leaning against the table, she gripped it hard and tried not to topple sideways. She sank onto the bench, searching for the creature.

Then she saw a brightness that was whiter and starker than moonlight. It was coming from the dish. She peered into the water. A light sat on the dish's bottom. It was as round and small as a pearl. Margot leaned close. "Who are you?" she asked again.

"Traveling on land makes me tired, and your language is so awkward. To you, I'm the bragha who's supposed to come when Ariana Elin's book calls. Then I'm supposed to transport you if you wish. Not from here, though. You'll have to get to the water."

Margot wanted to ask many questions all at once. "Transport me where?"

The whispering voice said nothing at first. Then the light, the bragha, went on. "I can show you better in my language." It traveled under the water, slowly, as if going a long way. When it reached the edge of the dish farthest from Margot, the water rose up before it. The water sprang from the dish and fanned out. It stretched high and wide, hanging like a woman's broad veil pinned to a wash line. As Margot watched, amazed, the water veil bent and stretched farther. It encircled her, forming a round room with her in the center. She saw now that the veil wasn't smooth; it was made of tiny droplets. The droplets lightened into whites, creams, and yellows. They darkened into blacks and browns, blues and purples. They became a mosaic.

The colors sharpened, and the picture became clear. It showed a tiered cliff. At the edge of each of its jagged tiers were faint trailing lights. Some were still. Some moved slowly along the tiers' edges. The bragha, the flickering light, swam through the droplets. It traveled up the tiers. The faint, eerie lights glowed as it neared them, then dimmed as it went by. Halfway up the cliff, it stopped. To look more closely, Margot stood, careful not to brush against and break the veil of droplets.

Eerie lights shone in the shape of a rounded door. On it, tiny iridescent droplets formed the same kind of oddly shaped letters that had once been in her book. They made a name she didn't recognize: ASRAI. "Asrai," she whispered. The sound of the word spoken aloud made Margot feel as if she'd heard a haunting, beautiful song. It gave her chills.

She turned slowly in a circle. She took in the whole mosaic, all the cliff's edges and lights. She studied the long wandering path the bragha had traveled. She wanted to step onto that path, stretch out her hand, and open the door.

"What is Asrai?" she asked, staring hard at the mosaic, so that when she closed her eyes she might see it on the inside of her eyelids.

"Come to the water. And don't, this time, bring he who's taken the book. He pries. I can feel him using his magic to learn from the book; those in Asrai may help you if you wish to win it back. Find me in the Sea," the creature whispered again, re-forming into the small flutter of wings. The water splashed down in a circle around Margot. The mosaic was gone. The bragha darted away, out the window.

Exhaustion weighed Margot down. She dropped back onto the bench and put her head on the table despite the dampness. She closed her eyes. Water in the blood didn't simply mean she had a book that told her things. She had magic inside her, as Orrin had suspected. Magic, inside her. The light was called a bragha and maybe had known Ariana Elin of Isles, one of the women whose names were in her book. It would take her to

Asrai—to those who might help her get her book back—if she could escape.

She didn't rise. Her fatigue must be the magic weariness people felt when they'd done too much too fast. Not that she'd really done much.

She drifted. She was falling asleep and couldn't stop. She could still see the craggy cliff in her mind's eye, and she could see the door she had to find.

A tapping woke Margot. She lifted her head. The room was black. Was it the same night, or had she slept through to the next one? She couldn't tell.

The tapping sounded again. "Lady?" whispered a voice.

It came from the window. She stared at the dark shape of the hinged window and the sky beyond. People even sought answers from her while she was locked up. "I don't want to talk," she said. "Go away."

"Quiet, or you'll wake the swordsman at the front. I haven't come for questions. I thought you might want a story," said the voice.

Margot glanced at the glowing coals and the shadowy walls. She was awake, not in some ridiculous dream. She went to the window and whispered, "A story? Did you say you thought I might want a *story*?" She couldn't have heard right.

"It's Bird, and I did."

"What do you mean, a story?" she demanded. He didn't like Orrin, Orrin didn't like him, and she didn't like either of them. "I'm locked in."

"I know," he answered. "You don't feel good, I hear. Although you have a swordsman instead of an herbalist at your door."

She could hear a smile in his voice. She wanted to drive it,

*143*

and him, away. This wasn't a joke. "What if there are swords-men because I was trading with demon spirits?" she said, try-ing to shock him.

"Were you?" The smile had left, though it was only replaced by interest.

He didn't sound as if he was teasing her. Still, she felt teased, poked at and examined for a laugh. "Why does the king dislike you? What have you done?" she asked, poking back.

There was a silence. She thought he'd gone. Then he said, "Orrin forbids stories. Without any regret." The voice was hard but not as angry as she'd expected. "He says it's for the best, that silencing some will help make fewer criminals. I think he's wrong. And I think he might really forbid them be-cause he doesn't like them. He only likes ones where good is all good and bad is all bad. But people aren't that way. He over-steps, demanding we can't tell and hear tales of how people truly are.

"So I don't praise and thank him. He's noticed. He's always noticed things like that.

"It seems you and he also disagree about something. And I wondered," Bird continued, his whisper sounding closer and sly in that storyteller's way, "if you might want to hear the tale you asked for the other night. The forbidden one, 'Gwist and the Pirate'?"

He wasn't laughing at her. He was doing this to stand against Orrin. She didn't know if he was right about the for-bidden tales, but the idea of standing against Orrin actually made her smile a little. "Why offer?" she asked, curious. "How do you know I won't tell him, after?"

"Would you?" he asked, still sly. But he also sounded trou-bled. He must have really missed speaking that story if he'd risk coming here and offering it.

A shiver went down the back of her neck.

If she asked for the tale, Orrin wouldn't have everything all his own way tonight. Bird would speak the stories he liked, not what Orrin said he could; she would listen to what she chose, not what Orrin said she could hear. "I won't tell him about you. I want 'Gwist and the Pirate.' But can I hear another first? Is 'The Lad and the Giant' one of the stories of your line?"

"It is," he said. The unease was gone from his voice. The smile was back.

He began, simply saying the words without the illusions. She leaned against the wall with her head close to the window.

The faceless words coming through the opening, their lilt and whisper, caught her up. They carried her with the boy. He was in a marsh that smelled of rot. He was in the giant's stinking, bloodstained hut. He was running with gold in his hands. Then he was in the heart's wood tree, hiding and tricking the giant.

Like the boy, the thief, the hero, her heart jumped below her ribs. Like him, she was clever; she was strong; she would escape to the bragha and Asrai.

# Eighteen

day and night passed. Then another.

Margot paced. She didn't stand still much. Not if she could help it. When she did, the walls seemed to close in on her. She'd remember confiding in Orrin or kissing him, and she'd want that "before" back with a miserable, mortifying intensity. Then she'd remember him holding her book high, out of her reach. The "before" wasn't really him. The stolen book, the locked door—*those* were really him. She'd want to knock over the bench and table. Tears would rise up and she'd force them down. She'd think of Asrai, which was a Western Isle, maybe, or a hidden place where many people like her lived; she was certain no one would think her tainted or try to use her there. She'd forget and go too close to the window. The wind would reach out to her. It smelled like Sea and freedom. She'd start thinking of mad ways to get out. She could scrape at the stone with her fingers. She could gnaw at the wooden door.

Night again, or no, almost dawn.

"Lady." The lilting voice was at the window. It came at night to tell her stories of women pirates or clever fishermen's wives. It made the room disappear, for a time. She knew it, the voice, belonged to Bird, but she didn't think of it that way. It seemed to be only sound, made of air and water.

"I'm sorry I wasn't able to get here earlier," Bird went on.

She should tell him to go, to drift away on the breeze. The sky was starting to lighten at the edges, and the guard would come in soon with food. Instead, she asked, "Do you have stories you've made? Would you tell me one?" When he was here, being near the window wasn't so difficult. So she leaned on the wall next to it.

He was silent, then said, "When I was small, I thought shaping new stories would be easy." He sounded as if he was laughing at himself. "Now I think of words but they don't fit together."

"When they do, come and tell them to me," she said, though it made her smile to think of him finding her the way a person would. He was just wind rippling through an open window.

"My thanks, but I might lose all my teeth and hair by the time they fit," he said, sounding like an old man. "You might be a crooked old woman. You might be deaf in one ear."

She laughed softly. She always had to be careful. She hadn't seen Orrin since he'd locked her in, but she wouldn't be surprised if he listened at the door. "Then you'll have to speak up," she replied.

His quiet laugh was like tricky Gwist's. Then he whispered, "You haven't let me tell you why I wasn't here before. There's a key to your door. I've been looking for it."

A key. She didn't want help from anyone, not even from the voice at the window, but she'd take it. To leave, she'd take it. "Can you find the key?"

"Yes," he whispered. "I have to leave."

He was gone. The small house was quiet. She edged away

from the window and the reaching wind. There was a key. But the door wasn't open yet.

✢

Night was gone, but the clouds were thick. The room was grayer than usual. Someone knocked, a swordsman with food and water. He barely looked at her; she couldn't tell how Orrin had explained the lock on the outside of the door. She made her face blank, just wanting him gone. He placed the tray on the floor, exchanged the crapping pot for a fresh one, and then shut her in again. There was a pitcher of water on the tray. Seeing it almost made her glad.

She went to the pitcher. As she neared it, she began to shake, eager to reach out and begin. The bragha hadn't returned. When she wasn't too tired, however, she still took water in her hands. She didn't understand what this magic's purpose was. She'd ask the bragha or those she met in Asrai if she reached it. No, not if. When.

She brought the tray to the table. Then she closed her eyes, looking for the place inside her that was a calm pool. She breathed in and breathed out, searching. When she found it, she opened her eyes and poured the water into the dish beside the pitcher. Then she scooped up water. Her hands warmed as she rolled it gently between her palms. It cleaved together, its surface like the smooth, delicate shell of an egg.

She had learned, since the bragha had come, how to make the water curve and flatten. She now knew how to mark it with cracks or letters. Though the bragha had given her only that one glimpse of the door and the word *Asrai*, the memory of what they looked like shone inside her so clearly. Paying close attention to that shining memory, she held the water with one hand. The other began to shape it. The heel of her palm sculpted. Fingertips pressed. Fingernails scored.

148

The water took the form of the cliff. It was awkward in some parts, too like water and not so like rock, but it had the right shape. She made the door and pressed in the letters—ASRAI. The small likeness wasn't as lovely and real as the memory in her head. Regardless, its clear water gleamed iridescent. It glittered and sparkled. She held it high and felt as if she, too, were gleaming and sparkling.

Half of her thought that the bragha would come this time and show her more. Half of her didn't care if it appeared or not. She was shaping water. She was wielding a magic her mother and the other women might have wielded, her magic.

Weary tremors began to quiver through her, which meant she should let the water go. She held it, though, just to have a few more gleaming moments. Then it broke and splashed down.

Tremors shook her knees. They weren't as bad as they'd been the first night, but they were bad enough that she knew she wouldn't shape again until much later. She almost hated the too brief feel she'd had of the water. Now all she could do was walk the length of the room. She went back and forth, dragging her hand against the stone wall. The strength to shape again, as well as night and the voice at the window, were thousands of steps away.

Her fingers scraped against the stones. Her steps were jerky with fatigue. She picked up the silver arm ring. She might need to wear it, to trick Orrin. She put it on, pulled it off, put it on. She stared at her boots, and then the door opened again.

Orrin came in and stopped. The sight of him was like a bright flash in darkness. She was caught in the flash, startled and speechless.

"You've had time to think." His expression was so certain. "Will you come out and tell us everything?"

He wasn't sorry at all. Inside, her chest suddenly felt raw and bruised. She hated that it did.

"Well?" he asked. His face was pallid.

If she told him about the stories she listened to at the window, he'd grow paler. He'd be angry and hurt. He'd know she wasn't going to give in. But that wouldn't help her escape.

Shamming repentance would get her outside. It might give her the chance to sneak away, and then she wouldn't have to accept the voice's help and the key. Still, she couldn't stand to let Orrin think he'd won.

But she had to. She forced her mouth to open and say the humiliating words: "I'll tell you everything you want to know."

Orrin nodded, watching her. "Before," she'd liked when he did that. She'd smiled and had probably looked like a begging puppy, desperate to be loved. Her jaw stiffened. She looked at her feet so he wouldn't see she was no longer begging.

They walked out, and swordsmen joined them. The smell of water and blustery wind wrapped around her. It made her want to run without a plan, just run. Which would get her nowhere. She couldn't fail; she couldn't let him win.

People rarely used the holy men's tunnel to the castle because the walk was short, but Orrin led her to the tunnel entrance. As they went down the poorly lit stairs, she studied his face. He looked righteous, as if it were noble to take her underground rather than walk in the Sea-scented air, to make her do something he must know she didn't like. She kept walking, her face blank.

She thought about standing on a table and telling the whole feast hall they might think he hadn't cried when he'd been teased as a boy, but he had. He'd hidden behind the hen house near the kitchen, and he'd sobbed. She savored the thought, and, unlike him, she knew what it honestly was: meanness, spite.

They arrived in the corridor between the entrance and the

kitchen. She saw no escape there, and none as she entered the feast hall. The swordsmen stopped by the door. At the high table sat Meynard and another holy man, platters of bones in front of them. Before them, an illusion of an old king shifted and faded, leaving Bird, and a glow waning from his hands. Margot stared at Bird as he spoke the tale's last words. His voice was familiar, but not his black braided hair or his long face. It didn't seem as if he could really have told stories at her window. She stared elsewhere, at Orrin's broad back. Bird said and did unexpected things: that wasn't what she needed now.

"Stop here," commanded Orrin, pointing to a lower table. Without explanation, he went to the holy men and began whispering to them. Standing and waiting while they looked her over was humiliating. Orrin watched her, as if making sure that she knew she deserved to wait and be shamed. He must think shaming her noble, too.

She ignored him. Wind from the few open windows twined in her hair and around her arms. It tugged her toward the windows. She took a few small steps toward the glass panes.

Thick gray clouds hung over rough Sea. Foam frothed on the sand, and farther out, too, where waves broke before hitting the shore. The water crashed and thundered. A storm was coming. Margot folded her arms so they wouldn't reach out one of the open windows. This wasn't the way to escape. She might not find one. She had to, quickly.

"Lady," the voice, Bird, said close to her. He bowed, but his mouth twitched with a fleeting mischief. "I'm glad you're better. We were all worried when the king said you were ill."

"My thanks," she answered, without warmth. It was disconcerting to hear that voice come from him, Bird, and she had no time for mischief now.

"Rest is the key, I've found," he said. No one listening would think he was talking about anything other than her health, but his expression was grave. "The key."

He'd found it.

He'd risked himself to find the key for her. His face was weary from staying up nights telling her stories. His tired eyes offered her help.

She wanted his help. She wanted him gone. Orrin had offered help, too. She'd very easily, very stupidly, taken it.

She was so slow to answer, his eyes grew troubled. He was worried over her. She gave him a false smile. "Have you?" she asked, pretending not to understand what he really meant.

"Everyone out," said Orrin. Margot flinched without meaning to and looked over at him. He rose fast. "Except Meynard, Bird, and the Lady. Wait behind the door." His voice was furious. The swordsmen and holy man didn't hesitate.

Margot tensed. Had he understood what Bird had truly said? Or was this a new part of the test? A new humiliation?

Bird bowed, but his shoulders had that unbending resentment Margot had seen in them before. He said, "Highness. Is something wrong?" She realized he'd put himself between her and Orrin and Meynard. She stepped up beside him, refusing his protection.

"I won't have you make a fool of me in front of anyone. I saw," accused Orrin. "I saw you this moment, standing so close, staring at each other. After the chance I've given you to right things. I've never given anyone such a chance," he said to Margot. "Him? You've chosen him instead of me?"

"What are you talking about?" Outrage made her speak too loud.

"You're mistaken, Highness," Bird said.

"I don't think he is," said Meynard, studying them both with distaste.

Margot stepped away from Bird and toward Orrin. "I barely even know him." She emphasized each word, but Orrin wasn't listening. He never listened. "I chose you. And you weren't giving me a chance, you were trying to make me tell you about water and magic."

"As you should," Orrin said. "And as you would, if you'd really chosen me. You'd tell me anything I asked. I was a fool not to judge and condemn you the other day." He looked down his hooked nose at Bird. "Because I so respected your father, I let you mourn and stay for now, though you aren't the tale teller he was. But clearly you haven't really been mourning. You've been skulking off to talk with her. Secretly. While she's betrothed to me. I'll rule you disgraced, or worse, condemned."

A howling made them all go still. Outside, the storm had finally arrived. Wind rushed in the windows, whining. Margot moved first: she was finished letting Orrin have say over her.

She kicked the lower windows as hard as she could. Shards of glass crashed around her boot and fell to the floor. Rain pelted in, riding on the back of howling wind, which broke more of the cracking, jagged windows. Men yelled around Margot, but she couldn't hear what they were saying. The glass now had a large opening. Margot felt as if her blood had caught fire. Heedless of sharp edges, she climbed out the opening and began to run.

# Nineteen

he wind and rain rushed in the broken windows. The Lady rushed out. Bird started to run after her. He'd visited her and offered her forbidden tales because he thought she might want to hear them. He'd also done it as a kind of leap, like plunging into an unfamiliar river pool. He'd enjoyed going. She and he laughed at the same stories. So he'd put off returning to Sharp Maud's alley and had told the Lady tales instead.

He didn't want Orrin to catch her, or him. He reached the broken window and glanced back at Orrin and Meynard. Orrin's hands glowed shockingly bright. They looked as though they had lightning trapped inside them, ready to strike a demon spirit. Meynard's face was unsurprised, but Bird wanted to shove Orrin and demand an explanation. He wasn't a demon spirit, and the Lady wasn't a demon spirit. Who knew what that magic might do if it touched them? Then Orrin came forward, the lightning in his hands flaring. He reached in Bird's direction. Bird stumbled over splintered glass and climbed through the hole.

He passed the garden gate. Above it, branches of heart's wood and blackspine lashed in the wind. The Lady was racing down the hillside's stone steps, which were slick with rain.

One falsely placed foot could send her tumbling, but she hurtled down anyway. He raced after her. He slipped. Cursing, he caught himself before he fell.

The Lady reached the bottom and jumped to the slate path. He expected her to run toward the larger rocks or the cliffs and hills beyond, but she didn't. She ran straight to the Sea. He jumped, too, looking to see if she was trying to reach a boat. No boat was out in the heaving waves. Then he saw something. Not on the water but in it, within a wave. There was a light, a blooming star of light.

As a child he'd wanted to know what secrets the Sea might whisper, secrets like what the seal's cries meant. He'd listened hard, then had grown up and stopped. Seeing the light made him long to hear those secrets like a child again, with real hope and a heart that seemed so close to the air that it hurt.

The Lady ran into the waves. She headed toward the light as if she'd been expecting to find it. He plunged in after her. Rain struck at him. The water banged against his lower legs and threatened to knock him down. The Sea storm could swallow them whole. Orrin was behind them. The blooming light shone; Bird couldn't look away from it. "Wait. Stop," he cried. She did, and he said, "Are you running toward the light? Can we reach it?"

"Do you want to reach it?" she asked, sounding surprised. Then she stared beyond him. "What is he doing?" she yelled.

Bird turned. Orrin was rushing down the steps with Meynard and a few swordsmen. Orrin's hands were too bright to look at. Their light was stronger than it had been, and different from the one in the water; it looked as if it could slice rock, sever bone. "I don't know." Orrin hadn't awed Bird before now. "I've never seen anything like it."

Orrin stepped down the final stairs. The Lady stood unmoving. Then she cried, "Swim," as she dived.

A flash like lightning streaked from Orrin and hit Bird's shoulder. Numb, he half dived, half fell. The water took him in. Pain burst in his shoulder and shot down his arm into his chest. The Lady and the light were before him in the rough gray water. He swam hard, but his arms and legs hurt. His chest hurt. Stories were far away, hard to remember.

~⑨~

Ahead of Margot, the light radiated uneven spokes of luminescence. She swam forward and downward, deeper into the gray-green water. Though it was cold and rough, it welcomed her. It ran over her like many hands, kneading at her weary muscles. It sped around her and bore her along. She kept swimming, helping it carry her toward the light, the bragha.

Nothing was quite as she'd planned. Orrin had chased them with a strong magic; he had her book; Bird was behind her. He'd said, "Can we reach it?" "We" again, as Orrin had once said to her. She didn't need the storyteller or the way his lilting voice wrapped around her.

The light was near now, glowing in the dim Sea like a fallen moon. It didn't move, only hovered. Margot's swimming faltered. What if it wouldn't lead her to Asrai while Bird was with her? What would she do then? The water streaming all around made turning her head difficult, but she looked back at Bird. She stopped swimming altogether. He was drifting nearby, as deep within the Sea as she was. The water carried him forward, but his head hung down and his arms floated at odd angles. His body looked like something tossed away and abandoned. She reached through the streaming water and snatched his wrist. It was limp, and burned as if with fever. Orrin's magic must have reached him somehow. At this moment, he might be sucking water into his lungs.

She didn't want him here, but she didn't want him to die.

She dragged him close. His wrist burned in her hand. Her own chest craved air. The light's brilliant beams reached out. It hovered. It was waiting. Waiting for what? She didn't know, couldn't think.

Her aching chest took over. It forced her booted feet to kick toward air. She reached down with her free hand, stretching so that her fingertips might brush the light. *Please. Stay there,* she thought, willing it to hear. *Or follow me.*

The light didn't rise to meet her fingers. It spun, and Margot was certain it would disappear. The words *Don't go,* cried within her.

The light darted down. Instead of leaving, it went beneath her and Bird. It touched her legs, then pushed her upward. She broke through the surface into the raging wind. Water swelled and plunged around her. Foam and rain struck at her cheeks. They went up her nose. She choked and held tight to Bird's wrist. Water splashed into her mouth. Its saltiness stung her tongue.

Then she rose higher, lifted from beneath until she was entirely out of the water. Her legs straddled something broad and smooth. She looked down, thunderstruck.

She was on the back of a brilliant white horse, with Bird slung before her like a sack, belly down. She let go of Bird's wrist and gripped a handful of his cloak. His shallow, unsteady breaths rose and fell under her knuckles. The horse was the luminescent white of the light and the feathery bragha that had visited her room. The rain still struck at her, but the shining horse rode high on the waves. Its whole neck and body were out of the water, so the Sea couldn't slap her or Bird. The creature craned its neck, as a real horse would, to regard her with one ivory eye. The eye was more ancient and wild than any other she'd seen. Looking into it was frightening, and wondrous.

She slowly reached out with her free hand and wound her

fingers in the mane. It felt like fine, silky horsehair. "My thanks," she said.

"I'll take you to Asrai," whispered the voice that was like water against sand. "You could drop the one with tale-teller magic in him into the water. Or, if you wish, I can help him as well. I like tale tellers. I like to watch them tell stories."

Margot felt the shallow breaths against her knuckles. She wasn't going to just drop Bird in the water to die or be captured by Orrin. "He's coming."

The creature tossed its head like any horse eager to be off. Then it jumped forward. Instead of swimming, it seemed to run. Margot held the folds of Bird's cloak and looked back.

Orrin was a tall dark figure at the shoreline, lightning streaking from his hands. The lightning disappeared before it reached them, though, as if he didn't have the strength to get it to them. Another figure beside him, Meynard, was bright with magic, too. Each of the horse's rocking strides carried Margot and Bird farther than any stride should, so the men on the shore quickly shrank to insignificant specks. Orrin had lost her. She wanted to see his face, just for one brief triumphant moment.

As she straightened, her boot bumped Bird's dangling hand. He hung unmoving, his black cloak like a shroud. He could still die because of Orrin. And Orrin still had her book. The rain and wind seemed to blow more bitterly. "How is my book? Can I get it back? Will we get to Asrai soon?"

"The land king tries to loot its magics, but it's fighting him. You may be able to get it back. I don't know." The horse flattened its ears. "Ask in Asrai. We'll get there soon enough for you, and perhaps for the tale teller as well."

"What's the matter with the storyteller? Is he dying?" Margot asked. Saying it made outrage surge through her. He couldn't die, he couldn't let Orrin beat him.

The bragha gave her one quick glance with its ancient, wild eye. "I'm no oracle, and I don't like talking so much in your clumsy language. You'll find your answers when you arrive." It tossed its head and fell silent.

Margot wanted answers now. The bragha hadn't even explained who Ariana Elin was, or how and why it had known her and the book. She imagined what that eye would look like when it was angry, though, and didn't push any harder.

She watched for some sign of their destination. The day seemed longer than any day should last. The horse galloped on and on. Margot's hair grew heavy. Her legs stiffened and cramped. She began to have difficulty judging where her fingers ended and the things they held began. Her stare fixed on the horse's back and on Bird. Gray-green water below, white back, black cloak.

Then the horse stopped. Her thoughts jerked out of their bleary haze. She looked up.

Before them, a huge rock jutted out of the Sea. It was just the tip, but it was brown-black and jagged edged: the cliff the light had shown her. The rest of it must be underwater. She could feel the pulse in her neck throbbing.

The horse gave a gentle shake. Then it sank into the water with a swiftness that startled Margot. The mane melted from her fingers. The horse's head shortened and rounded, and the creature dived away. It took Bird with it and left her alone as the Sea dragged at her leaden clothes, boots, and limbs. Then the rounded head, a glowing white seal's head, popped up near her. It was seal shaped but not a seal person such as Orrin had talked of. Behind it bobbed several more glowing seals' heads. These creatures were belly-up in the water; they formed a circle. Bird lay, face to the sky, on their bellies. His skin was as yellow as an old man's, and the wet hadn't woken him. She wished he weren't sick or even here, but he'd have to come with her. She looked back at the rock. "Let's go," she said.

Her tired strokes were clumsy. The Sea tugged her hard, and even floating was difficult. The seals carrying Bird gave her impatient nods. Margot's seal dived and came up beneath her, supporting her chest. "Thank you," she said, still staring at the rock. She wrapped her arms around the seal's neck and said again, "Let's go."

"Take a deep breath and hold it," whispered the bragha. Margot breathed in, realizing the other seals and Bird weren't on the surface anymore. Then the seal took her under, down, down, down. She had to clasp her numbed hands together. The water slid past her too fast, running through her hair and inside her clothing. It grew colder and darker each moment. Lights shone here and there, but they were only blurs in the green-black water. Margot's shivering made her teeth chatter. Her fingers slipped, and she gripped harder. Her head buzzed with the need for air.

The seal went through something that clung and slid over them like an invisible curtain. Then the curtain let go as the bragha dragged them onto a ledge. Margot clambered off; she was no longer surrounded by water. She leaned against the cliff and sucked in air. Just louder than her breathing was a brushing sound. It seemed to be the Sea moving against the invisible barrier that held it away from the side of the cliff. Bird lay still by her feet. She crouched and touched his chest. Fever heated his drenched tunic, and his chest rose and fell, slightly. He hadn't given in yet.

A throaty, trilling voice sounded near her. It was speaking nonsense. No, it spoke words. "Who trespasses here?"

Margot looked up to a woman. Her answer stuck in her throat. She'd never before looked at someone and seen her own features. This woman was the same height as Margot, and her face had the same shape, too thin. She also had very pale skin, so pale it looked as if it had never been in the sun's light. Her hair was black and straight. From the eerie glow of a glass lantern, Margot could see that the woman's eyes weren't black like hers. They were large and brown, with long dark lashes. Margot wanted to touch the face, feel that it was real. Here was someone who must be like her, who must have water in her blood. Margot forced an answer out of her throat. "I was brought here from the westlands. He comes from there, too. He's sick. He needs help." She looked for the bragha and its companions. They weren't on the ledge or out beyond the invisible barrier, in the green-black Sea. They had left her.

Then she noticed something beyond the woman. A string of lights illuminated the darkness. They were in the cliff, around a stone door. On the door was an iridescent word of lovely, strange letters: ASRAI. Margot stood.

The woman held up an odd staff that had curled ends. Beneath her fur cloak was a long-bladed knife belted around a simple blouse and what looked like men's loose riding trousers. "You don't have a better answer?" She had an odd way of pausing before she spoke, as if she measured what she said carefully. "Demon spirits might have sent you. To get me to open the door."

It took Margot a moment to decipher the strange-sounding words. "They didn't," she said with a dread she hadn't felt since she'd ridden through the midlands. Here, she'd have to fear demon spirits again. "I'm sorry, I can explain better. The man's ill, and I've been searching for that door for a long time." She spoke fast. "Braghas brought me."

The woman's staff moved down slightly. She hesitated again, gathering her words. "Braghas? Really? What's your name? How did they bring you?"

Margot thought this was a test. She had to give the right answer. She interlaced her fingers behind her and talked more slowly. "I'm Margot of Pristanne, the daughter of Maira Alys of Isles of Pristanne." She briefly explained how she'd traveled to this ledge. The woman kept shooting looks down the path, into the dark. Margot couldn't tell if she was listening or only pretending to as she kept watch for demon spirits. Finishing, Margot said, "I'm supposed to go through that door."

The woman frowned as if troubled. "You're of the Land?"

Margot's soaked clothing seemed to grow colder. She didn't know how she was supposed to answer. "Bird is a story-teller from the westlands—"

"A tale teller? I didn't realize." The woman bowed her head and pressed her fingertips to her forehead. It seemed to be a sign of respect. Then she gave a shrill whistle. A man and a woman, who were dressed as she was, came from different places on the path. "The tale teller needs healing," she said urgently as they also gave him the odd bow. They knelt and began to gently pick him up.

"And you?" asked the woman. "Why are you here? Answer quickly."

"I've lived in the westlands, but I can't anymore." The woman still didn't welcome her. "Back there, where I've lived, it's very rare to understand water. I do, but I've never met anyone else who does. The rest either try to use me because of what I know, or sneer at me." Margot had never wanted so desperately to say the right thing.

The woman shook her head and muttered something that sounded like "Land Creepers."

Margot froze; she didn't know if the woman meant her. "Pardon me? I didn't quite hear you."

The woman shook her head again and said, "It was nothing." She yanked her knife free. Then she said to Margot, "When I open the door, go in quickly. If the demon spirits come, I'll leave you out here for them to grab. If they don't, the chieftain will want to speak with you."

Margot felt giddy. "They won't. Not because of me," she said. Talking to the chieftain would be the next test, but she'd passed this one. She could barely keep still.

The woman pulled the door open. As the others carried Bird through the doorway, she gave a quick bow. "I, Esyllt, gatekeeper to Asrai, invite you and your storyteller in as guests. Now hurry."

Margot stepped into a softly lit corridor. Her feet were light. They hardly seemed to touch the ground.

# Twenty

syllt and Margot went down one corridor. The gatekeepers carrying Bird went down another. Lights hung from hooks in the walls. The brown rock around them had veins of white, yellow, and red. All Margot's searching and longing had led her to these moments. She'd been meant to find this corridor, this land. The chieftain Esyllt was taking her to would have to see that.

They rounded a corner, and Esyllt gestured for Margot to slow. "Quietly," the gatekeeper said. She pointed out crevices in the rock. "These go down deep. The demon spirits might hear, in their underground kingdom. They dig away and open them. We lost someone a few days ago."

Margot stepped away from the crevices. Esyllt turned into a long, narrow passage. At any small sound, she turned and stared hard at cracks in the wall. A tightness was in Margot's neck, the tension of always having to watch and be careful.

Regardless, her fear was so small compared to her excitement. She wasn't sure who the chieftain was or what he might ask of her. How had these people come here? Why hadn't her mother lived with them? She didn't know—yet. She just knew this was exactly where she was supposed to be.

They turned into another passageway. To one side, there were two holes in the floor, which were covered by some kind of clear rock. Inside the holes were water and light. The light shone on an underwater ledge that held round creatures with many small, thin arms. The creatures were a shade of pink so bright they seemed to shine. Several orange fish with eyes on the top of their heads flitted among the many arms. Black star-shaped creatures wrapped around what looked like stones or eggs. The next hole had more of these. It also had what looked like leafy plants, but they were as still as stones. The stone plants were red, green, and violet. Coral—Margot knew the name from her book—the kind that grew in cold, dark water. She wanted to lie on the floor, belly down, and stare.

The passage twisted. They walked past a ridged section of wall. A rush of chilly air pushed past them suddenly. It knocked Margot a little off balance. Then, from behind, came a thick white fog. Instead of feeling damp, it felt dry, and hot but not too hot. It also sent a sparking and spraying feeling across her skin.

Esyllt seemed unconcerned. Margot rubbed her hands together. The spraying fire feeling burned a little but wasn't painful. She didn't want to slow them, but she had to ask, "What is this?"

"It's only magic. It'll pass." Esyllt tilted her face into the mist, like someone basking in the sun.

It was very strange: the slight burning feeling, the magic all around them even though they weren't at a rite, the way Esyllt tilted her head. What was this magic here for? The holy man, whoever was calling it up, must be powerful; Margot couldn't see him anywhere near. Or her, she realized. Here, women like Esyllt fought. They might use magic as men did, too, and as she did. Maybe Esyllt was taking her to see this person, and maybe it was a woman. She tried to smooth her wet gown.

Then, without warning, the mist drifted by them. The sparking feeling went with it, leaving the passageway dim, cool, and empty. She and Esyllt were alone. No one was in the hall ahead of them.

Margot looked behind. No one was there, either. Could these people reach out with magic the way Orrin could? Perhaps they—women, too—were stronger than he was and could reach out farther. "I don't see the person calling up the mist," she said, hoping the gatekeeper would explain. She'd burst if she didn't get more answers soon.

"It's just magic bubbling up," Esyllt said. Margot had the disconcerting feeling that she must look the way Esyllt now did: her eyes were a little narrowed, as if she was thinking. "This never happens on the Land?"

"No," Margot answered, but then wasn't certain. The holy men might know times and places where it had. "I don't know. I thought magic was only in people or spirits. Is it in the ground? Or the Sea? It must be in the Sea," she answered herself, thinking of how the water had helped carry her.

"That's no secret," said Esyllt, shrugging. "Land boatmen avoid some places because the magic makes the water dangerous and unpredictable."

Margot didn't remember reading that in her book. Or maybe she'd read it but hadn't really understood what it meant. Regardless, she was learning now. "Is the magic in all water, or does it only come from certain places?" Margot asked. The questions rushed out of her. "Do you know when you might find it, or where?"

"Those are Sea secrets," Esyllt answered brusquely.

Margot faltered. She didn't want to offend or anger the

gatekeeper, especially now; she'd only just arrived. She had to be patient. She should speak more carefully. She'd even walk more carefully. She followed Esyllt, putting one foot directly in front of the other. She wouldn't stray to the left or the right. Esyllt would have no complaint to make to the chieftain.

Esyllt took her to a cavern with a sheer wall. The wall had a few doors, some on ledges above them. They went up a set of stone stairs. Esyllt pulled open a door and they entered a small room. It had a glass-encased light on a shelf, and also a window of what looked like clear, polished stone. A pallet lay on the floor. In a corner were a stone table and bench. The walls had a few shelves, also made of rock. Against one wall was a square trunk. Esyllt pulled a simple gray gown from the trunk, handed it to Margot, relocked the trunk, and said, "This is my room. Stay here. I'll go arrange your audience." Then she left.

Margot put on the dry gown and laid her wet one on the stone table. Then she didn't know what to do. She couldn't just sit.

She walked around the room, looking. The most interesting thing was the locked trunk. With one finger, Margot tapped the top of the leather-like lid. What would the gatekeeper have inside? Weapons? Jewelry? She had a hard time imagining Esyllt wearing jewelry. The gatekeeper walked like a swordsman. Her hands looked chapped and rough. She might wear rings the way a man would, but not dangling necklaces or earrings.

What was in the trunk really didn't matter. Margot glanced at the door. She listened for footsteps but didn't hear any. She had to be patient. She wondered if her book was safe and if people here would really help her get it back. She wondered if Bird was all right. He needed help, as did her book. Then there was her audience, where she'd meet the chieftain. Yet she was just here, doing nothing. Patient, she had to be patient.

She went over to the narrow pallet. The blanket was a kind of fur she hadn't seen before. It almost looked slick. Something beside the head of the pallet caught her attention. Half hidden by a corner of the fur, as if set down and momentarily forgotten, was a bird's nest.

Margot knelt and gently pushed aside the blanket. The nest was made of sticks and also had two strips of red cloth woven into it. The hollow held three small blue eggs. They were broken but not shattered. Esyllt or someone else must have found them soon after they were pushed from the nest, saved them, and taken the empty nest later. Margot sat back on her heels.

She glanced at the trunk. Maybe instead of jewelry it held dried wildflowers or feathers. People here might know far more about the shore, or even about her, than she or anyone on land knew about them. She readjusted the blanket so that it hid the nest. Soon she'd learn about them, too—if Esyllt ever came back. Why was she taking so long?

Margot fidgeted around the room until Esyllt finally returned. She said the chieftain and the family heads weren't ready for an audience. She didn't explain why, only that they'd gather soon. The way she said it made it sound as if they weren't all nearby. Esyllt paused in her odd way before saying, "Do you want to see the tale teller?"

It took Margot a moment to grasp what Esyllt had asked. "He's all right?" As Margot asked, she felt a tug, a pull to see him that she didn't like. She didn't want to be drawn to him, or anyone, the way she'd been to Orrin.

Nevertheless, she did want him to get well. "He's better?"

"No, but he's not worse," the gatekeeper said.

"Will he be all right?" Margot asked, more worried.

"I don't know," Esyllt said gravely.

"There's an herbalist with him? Someone who heals?" she asked. "What did he say?"

"A wisdom, yes," Esyllt told her. "He's not sure what will happen to the tale teller, either."

There was no one else who'd look in on Bird, who'd look after him. She could avoid him anyway, but that seemed mean. His coming to her window had made being locked in easier. Going would also fill up some time while she waited. "I'd like to see him," she said. She'd go, but she wouldn't stay long.

This time, as they walked, she noticed how empty and silent it seemed everywhere. There were all these passageways. Yet no voices echoed in front of or behind them. If Esyllt left her alone, she'd be lost in a moment. She saw no dropped or forgotten pieces of basket, strips of rag, or buttons, as one might in a street. The passages had the feel she remembered from the mountain borderlands, a lonely, half-wild feel. Whether this was because few people lived here or because guests were only guided through out-of-the-way places, she didn't know.

"Mora's people have taken him in," Esyllt said. "We're almost there."

Margot wasn't sure who or what "Mora's people" were. A family, perhaps, or an order, as "gatekeeper" seemed to be? She was nervous all of a sudden. There might be things they would or wouldn't expect her to say, things she knew nothing about. Or Bird might be more hurt and ill than he had been before.

They entered a room that was larger and rounder than Esyllt's. It had bigger polished-stone windows and was empty, like the passageways. Rolled furs lined the room's edges. More furs were spread on the floor like mats. Shelves held stones, many of them red or black. There were also shells. Margot marveled at a transparent one with long spikes and a large black one with a rounded pink lip and creamy inside. Nobody entered the room or greeted them. Like the rest of Asrai she'd seen, it had an empty feel. It smelled of salt, and also maybe of marsh sweetgrass, but faintly, as if someone had cooked and slept in the room days before, then left. She was almost certain the gatekeeper was taking her only to the outer edges of this place. But Bird was out here, too. So when he left, he wouldn't really know all that was in Asrai. Margot liked that he, and everyone else, would never see the place she'd left the west-lands for.

They went down a short passageway, through which she and the gatekeeper had to crouch to fit. Then they entered a cave-like room. It had one round window, as well as a stone table and bench. The lights, which hung on hooks, were small and dim. A bent old man, a wisdom, Esyllt had called him, sat against the wall. He wore a string of stones around his neck, and a plain tunic. Near him, Bird slept on a pallet.

Bird seemed thinner and faded. He was silent because he was sleeping, but Margot couldn't imagine him saying any-thing, even if he opened his eyes. Her breastbone hurt. He made her think of a forever-silenced harp, wood cracked, strings ripped out of place. "He won't get better?" she asked.

Like Esyllt, the wisdom hesitated before he spoke, as if words didn't come easily. "He could," the wisdom said. He cleared his throat with a bullfrog-like noise. "He might. He's your man?"

"No," Margot answered immediately. She edged farther away from the pallet. She didn't want a man, she just wanted him to be able to tell stories again. "No, but he's a good story-teller."

"There are many tale tellers on the Land," Esyllt remarked.

"But I liked listening to him." Margot realized she'd said *liked*. He wasn't dead. "I *like* listening to him."

"Wisdom?" The gatekeeper asked instead of responding to her.

The old man was standing, his head tilted. He seemed to be listening. "Rain's coming," he replied.

Margot noticed a low, misty cloud in the room. Then rain started falling. It had a shine to it that reminded Margot of diamonds; the drops were bright and caught hints of other colors. She felt that sparking burning again. But the rain was also soft. She could imagine it enticing flowers out of the hard brown rock.

The rain fell on all of them. Bird's forehead smoothed as if the drops were washing away a bad dream. The wisdom and Esyllt didn't try to find shelter. The man bent his head, as if he liked the rain's touch on the back of his neck. The gatekeeper held out one arm and watched the drops hit her palm. She let it run over her fingers and down her forearm.

Though still worried about Bird, Margot looked up so that the rain landed straight on her face. Here, she realized, magic wasn't something only storytellers, minstrels, herbalists, and holy men—especially holy men—used. It wasn't something a person stood in a handful of times a year, only at rites. Magic was all around, every day. It was bubbling up and pouring down. Margot closed her eyes and let it pour down on her.

# Twenty-one

argot slept alone in Esyllt's room. The gatekeeper woke her from an anxious sleep and told her to hurry. The chieftain was ready for her.

Her gown was wrinkled and still damp in spots. She pulled it on and tried to neaten it. She combed her hair with her fingers. Then she met Esyllt outside the room. "I'm ready," she said, her hands hidden behind her back. They were shaking.

Esyllt led her through passageways that seemed to go down forever. At one point rain fell around them. At another, Esyllt stopped. She pulled out her dagger, waited, then said, "I don't smell them." Margot assumed that "them" meant demon spirits, though how a dagger would fight them off she didn't understand.

After what seemed both too much and too little time, they reached a door. It had often-mended cracks. Esyllt pulled it open. Margot looked in, speechless.

The hall was small, the size one might find in a poor village lord's house. Lanterns of clear rock or glass were strung up, giving off soft, warm light. The walls and floor were polished opal-like stone. They were old, worn smooth.

She went forward. Three people sat at the head table, two women and a man. The man had very pale skin, which seemed rubbed thin by the years. He wore a simple blue tunic. Both women had black hair that was long, straight, and streaked with white. Their gowns were also simple and blue. They had many shells braided into their hair, and one woman also had pearls. They didn't speak, only stared back at her with large dark eyes. They were studying her. She belonged here. They had to see that.

The woman with the pearls said, "Whom do you present here, Esyllt, Gatekeeper?" Her voice was husky, and Margot had never seen any woman with such a strong, fierce face.

"I present the Land Walker I told you about, Chieftain," answered Esyllt. Margot started. This woman ruled here.

The woman asked Margot, "What is your name?"

Margot was transfixed by the face, which was somewhat like hers but framed by small braids of pearls. "I'm Margot of Pristanne, Chieftain."

The woman tilted her head. Her eyebrows arched. "That's not where you've lived." She gestured to Margot's arm. She paused, gathering her words, then said, "We watch the Land. You're wearing an arm ring I've seen before. You know Orrin of Mawr?"

Margot touched the silver fish wrapped around her arm. She'd kept it on so that Orrin wouldn't suspect she meant to run. Now she wished she hadn't. She didn't want to explain him. She didn't want to say anything that might upset or insult. But she couldn't lie to this woman who looked like her. "It belongs to Orrin of Mawr, Chieftain. We were betrothed," she said, searching the woman for some sign of approval or disgust and finding neither. Her mouth was dry. "Now I won't marry him. I won't ever live near him again." She slid the fish off and placed it on the table. Her arm felt weightless.

The other woman, the old man, and Esyllt all shifted. The chieftain gave a small tight smile. "Welcome, Margot of Pristanne. This is Mererid and Horas, the heads of their families. You've met Esyllt. And I'm Aerinwy, Chieftain of Asrai."

"I'm glad to meet all of you, Chieftain," Margot said, her mouth still dry. "Why did you ask if I knew Orrin?"

"One of the braghas came to me. He told me King Orrin had brought you to the westlands. He also said that you can shape water. I wanted to talk with you," Aerinwy answered. "Then the bragha didn't return right away, as if he'd lost you or couldn't get to you. And braghas often do as they wish, not what's asked of them. I wanted to be sure, in the end, he conveyed the right woman to me."

"You asked to speak with me?" Margot said. Did this mean the chieftain had hoped she'd come and live here? "Why?"

"We're used to holy men seeking us. Long ago, when we walked the Land more, they talked to us. They wanted to know what we knew about the Sea. They didn't ask us to tell them. They demanded. Or they spied on us.

"That is why we stay away from Land Walkers. Few have seen us. We've let fewer come here, to the outlands of Asrai. Despite this, many keep looking for Sea secrets. Orrin's stronger and more determined than most. Maybe his mother made him suspect we're here. She had some of our blood. Water in the blood, as it's called on the Land. It should have become diluted and disappeared. Instead, it skips through families and reappears in unpredictable ways," she said, sounding both proud and angry. "He wants the magics he believes are here. He's come close to finding us. You're no longer his ally. You might help us."

Margot tried to take in the chieftain's words. Few had seen these people. And she did have their blood. They were like her, as she'd thought. And Orrin wasn't just pushing her for answers, he was trying to reach this place. Everyone's eyes were on her. They were waiting for her to speak. "How could I help?"

Mererid, Horas, and Esyllt watched her. Aerinwy said, "You wouldn't have to do much. Just tell me when he'll ride the Sea next. Tell me the name of his boat and the dates of his travel. When you go back, would you find out and send us word?"

"And then you'll do what?" Margot barely heard herself. The chieftain had said "go back." She couldn't mean for good. "You don't want me to stay here? Or near here?" she asked.

"Stay?" asked Mererid, as if surprised. Horas smirked.

Aerinwy replied, "You could. Though your blood is quite tainted."

Margot hadn't heard that word in a long time; its teeth were still so pointed, its bite still so sharp. "Tainted?"

"With the blood of the Land," said Mererid, in a tone that suggested Margot was simple-minded. "You have no skin. Do you?"

"No what?" Margot asked, her tongue, her whole mouth stiff.

"Skin." Aerinwy gestured to a shell locket that hung on a thick chain around her wrist. They all had one, Margot saw, but the lockets were very small. What they held must be folded with magic. "Seal skin. So you can travel. And truly *swim*." The chieftain said "swim" the way someone might say the name of the person she loved. "Your Land Walker blood traps you in that shape. If you lived here, you'd have to stay in Asrai most of the time. The braghas aren't tame creatures. They won't cart you about. Would you miss basking in the sun? Or breathing free air?"

Margot did want sun, warm orange light on her face and arms. These people, with whom she shared blood in some way, were seal people. They weren't more like animals, as Orrin had said all those weeks before. They were people who had second skins, seal skins. They swam the Sea as seals. She wouldn't let herself imagine what having such a skin might be like. She didn't have one. She was not like them. Again, she was different. Again, she was tainted.

"Well?" Aerinwy asked.

Margot didn't answer. Tainted and unwanted. She would not let that be her. A heat kindled inside her. It wasn't the sun's gentle heat. It was a scorching, painful heat, full of fury. This was no home.

She'd find the place where she really belonged. The place her mother had come from: the Western Isles. As for the book, it had led her here. Or misled her. She'd take it back from Orrin. Then she'd bury it in a hole, under rocks and water, and walk away. "I'll tell you my decision later," she said. "I'd like to talk with the bragha who brought me. Is there a way to call him?"

Aerinwy gave her an odd look. "The way hasn't changed in the last few hours."

"I never asked him to bring me here," Margot said harshly. She paused. If she told them about the book, they might explain it. She didn't want to ask them for anything, though, not even an explanation. "He came on his own."

"When he first told me about you, he said he'd been called to the Land. You say not by you." The chieftain took in a long breath, then went on, speaking slowly and deliberately. "Do you have a book? A book called *The Book of the Sea*?"

They wanted it. Excitement brightened their large dark eyes. Not because of her, because of the book. "It's gone,"

Margot told them. She hoped this news hurt. "Orrin has it, and it's gone."

Excitement was replaced by shock. Horas cursed. Mererid shook her head. Esyllt thumped her staff on the floor and looked away. Margot felt a brief whisper of pleasure.

Aerinwy rose. She came around the table to Margot, moving with a graceful swiftness that seemed dangerous. Margot stood her ground. The chieftain said, "Margot of Pristanne, you're the true daughter of your mother's foolish grandmother."

"My mother's grandmother wasn't foolish," Margot said, refusing to let the chieftain know how little she'd heard of her mother's family. "You've no right to say that."

"I have every right. You don't know anything about her, do you? She was one of us. She married a man of the Land: this was the first foolish thing she did. She had a child by the Land Walker. A daughter, Tegwen. Then she abandoned the daughter because she couldn't bear to be away from here. However, she wanted the child and those of her line who carried her blood to have something of the Sea. Before she returned to us, she gave Tegwen a book, *The Book of the Sea*. She'd made it using magics no one knew she had the power to use. The book has the kind of secrets those with water in their blood know. At first, she said those secrets were all it had. That would have been bad enough. The fishermen, boat builders, and seal hunters take much from the Sea already; there shouldn't be more in the Land realms to help them. Especially the seal hunters, the butchers. But then, later, she admitted it had more. It doesn't tell of us directly, doesn't betray us in that way, yet there's the map. It senses each new master or mistress. When one nears the Sea, it leads him or her to us. Who knows what other magics or secrets she hid in that book? And she put them in the hands of Land Walkers: that was the second foolish thing she did."

Aerinwy gave a ferocious, mirthless smile. "That book has helped none of you. The Western Isles have been full of wars and chaos since then. Those of the Isles, more than other Land Walkers, seek us. More of them know that water in the blood means having some of our blood. Rival chieftains have always hoped to marry women like you. They want to discover a few water secrets—where best to fish, how best to build boats, where best to hunt the smaller seals—so that they might win more esteem. The chieftains all wanted Tegwen. She was stupid at first, and found ways to show off the book. They could tell it was a thing of great magic and wanted it. We tried to find her. We were going to demand that she give up the book, but she disappeared. Your mother was her daughter, I suppose, and wise enough to keep the book—and herself—hidden. Though not wise enough to come to us."

All heat drained from Margot. War, chaos, and rival chieftains fighting over a woman as starving dogs fight over a bone, that was the Western Isles. There was nowhere left that she might hope to go and find welcome. No other family. No other land.

Aerinwy looked down on her. "We mean to defeat Orrin. I know he wields his strong magic against demon spirits. But with it, he also searches for us, even though we don't want to be found. What if we refused to give him our secrets? Or what if he decided he should rule us? He might stop the plague of demon spirits here, but he would also take our secrets. He'd rule Asrai like any other Land Walker, without regard for our laws. If we defied him, he would use that magic against us.

"Think about whether you'll help us win the book away from him. Although maybe you can't undo the harm you've done. He might have already made it show him the map."

Margot didn't answer. If she spoke, if she breathed too deeply, she might break apart. Esyllt tried to take her arm. Margot pulled away. She was surprised to find she didn't crack into tiny pieces. Then she turned and started for the door.

～◎～

Bird opened his eyes. He ached all over. He was cold, despite the heavy blankets. Memories flashed through him, of breathlessness and of drowning. He'd also drunk a thick draft, poured for him by an ancient, wrinkled man. The Lady had leaned over him. His head throbbed as he shifted to see if she sat nearby. She didn't; no one did. What land were they in, and under whose care? He shifted again, grimacing as the throbbing and the aching grew worse. Then he looked for a bell or a way of calling someone for answers.

The strange room wasn't much bigger than the pallet he lay on. It was made of stone. One lantern hung above him on a hook. A stone table was bare. He tried to push himself up, but his vision went spotty. Pitching over and cracking his head open wouldn't help him. He lay back. His vision cleared.

How had he come here? He remembered falling into the water behind the Lady. There had been a bright luster, the light before them. Orrin's lightning had hit him. There'd been pain.

Bird gripped the edge of the blanket that lay over him. He'd already woken up, alone, in this room. He'd remembered all this before, and he'd realized the pain had damaged the place in him that held his stories. He'd lost a couple of them; he couldn't think of the words to "Gwist and the Beggar King" or "The Sealskin Girdle." Both stories had been old, passed down many generations from storyteller to apprentice. Only their titles and a few ragged phrases were left in him. They were only two, but still. This was worse than being forbidden from saying them; they were gone. He had failed his father. He was thinner, lesser, lacking.

As if brought on by these memories, a tightening started around his eyes. His body started to shake, recognizing the tightening before his mind did. It was the beginning of the stabbing pain. Now he was glad no one was near to see him. The pain would fill him. He feared it would blot out more tales.

This time, the pain didn't burst and rush. It grew slowly. Each moment dragged. Bird was so cold. The blanket and the pallet seemed to be made of ice. He had never thought holy-man magic stank before, but the pain, or the leftover bits of spell that had made the pain, smelled metallic. He wanted to cough it out the way a fortuneteller coughed out fire for coins.

Then he said, "Don't snail along. Finish." That he would urge the pain on struck him as funny. He laughed.

He hurt all over. He couldn't stop laughing. He couldn't get through the waiting.

A story.

His laughter ended abruptly. He could tell a story, just speak the words since he was too weak to weave magic. The pain might then blot out the very tale he spoke, but he would tell it anyway. He was thinner, lesser, lacking, but he was a storyteller.

*"There once was . . . A man went . . ."*

His whispering faltered. What story was that? Who was the man, and where did he go? A title swam up through him, "The Pirate Battle." That tale couldn't be gone, too; not that one. Pitching his voice louder, he began again.

*"Once there was . . . a pirate who everyone . . . feared . . ."*

The words stopped. The tale was gone. "The Pirate Battle" was gone. "Gwist and the Beggar King." "The Sealskin Girdle." "The Pirate Battle." Other storytellers told them, but not the way those of his line had. His line's tellings of these three stories were gone.

Bird shut his eyes. He didn't want to find a fourth hole where a story had been. The cold and the metallic stink gnawed at him.

There might not be a fourth hole, but he didn't start another tale. He began to hear something. It was a rhythmic beat, the footsteps of the gatekeeper of death. They were coming toward him. The gatekeeper would take him into the spirit court. He had no apprentice. His stories and his deeper storytelling magic would go with him, away from these lands forever. He'd have to face his father's spirit and explain.

But the beat now seemed to come from within him. It didn't sound like footsteps. It sounded like the rhythmic beat of water, waves. Clear, bell-like words formed in the waves, not words he'd ever learned or told. They were words to a new story, one shaped by him.

> *"A fisherman's boy once lived by the edge of the water.*
> *The boy had a wild heart,*
> *full of storms,*
> *and the laughing calls of birds*
> *and the whole wide unknowable Sea."*

He repeated the words so they'd reach that innermost well where all his stories lived. He could see the boy's face. The boy had sly brown eyes and a bent nose. He knew the boy wouldn't ever be happy until he left his mother and father's shack and traveled on the Sea.

The pain lessened. It eased and drifted away. Maybe Orrin's spell was wearing off, or maybe his own strength was fighting it off; he didn't know or care. He had found the beginning to the first story that was wholly his own: "The Fisherman's Boy."

# Twenty-two

argot lay on Esyllt's thin pallet, wrapped in the strange slick fur blanket. Once she left Aerinwy, she'd realized she had nowhere else to go. So she'd come back here. She'd slept. Now she was awake. Outside the polished-stone window, the Sea was black. No night, no day.

She curled on her side, knees to chin. She'd always thought there was a place that she'd walk into and fit, as all others seemed to fit somewhere. She was sure that the moment she reached it, she'd know it was hers. That place didn't exist.

She curled tighter. Ariana Elin of Isles, Tegwen Lassair of Isles, Maira Alys of Isles of Pristanne—the names whirled in her, carving out emptiness. Ariana Elin of Isles had abandoned her own child. Tegwen Lassair of Isles had fled and disappeared. Maira Alys of Isles of Pristanne had been a mixed-blood woman, landless, an outcast. Margot had never felt so empty. A wind might tear her into many shreds and scatter her. She wished one would.

A bell rang, sounding from above the door. Margot didn't move. If she lay still enough, she might just become emptiness. Whoever was behind the door would come in and find no one.

"Margot of Pristanne," Esyllt's voice said. "I've got food and drink."

"I'm not hungry," Margot replied.

There was a long silence; then Esyllt said, "I thought, since the queen said you shape water . . . I brought water for you to shape. If you want to."

Margot felt something leap inside her that wasn't emptiness. The emptiness swallowed it. "I don't need anything."

"Margot of Pristanne, I'd like to talk with you." Esyllt sounded determined. "May I come in?"

Margot pulled the blanket over her face. She could tell the gatekeeper to go away, and then she would have to listen later. Or she could listen now and be done with it. She got up, went to the door, and let Esyllt in.

Esyllt carried another, stronger light and a tray with several large polished shell dishes. She arranged the tray on the stone table and hung the light on a hook with impatient swiftness. Margot could smell cooked, spiced fish. She could also smell salt water, Sea water. She didn't go to the tray, though. "What do you want?" she asked.

Esyllt gestured to the tray. "Before we talk, you should eat. Or at least sit. You don't look good."

"I'm fine. I'd rather stand. What do you want?" Margot repeated.

Esyllt nodded. She took even more time to speak than she usually did. "I'm your cousin. A grandchild of one of the children Ariana left behind when she went to the Land. I wanted—" She stopped, then started again. "I've always wondered about *The Book of the Sea.* I wanted to know if you'd tell me more of it."

"A cousin?" A silent shadow of a laugh twisted through Margot. She'd been searching for her mother's family and she'd found it; here was another cousin who'd sneer at her, just like Isabeau and the rest. "It taught me about water. It called a bragha so I could come here. There's nothing else to tell."

Esyllt frowned. "You must know more than that."

"I don't," Margot said. There, they were done. Esyllt would go.

Instead, the gatekeeper said, "The book showed you how to shape water."

Margot wanted Esyllt gone, but she also felt the something leap in her again. "It didn't," she replied without really intending to. "Do people here shape water? How did they learn?"

"We don't. It's something only mixed bloods, those with water in their blood, can do," Esyllt said. She talked with a kind of passion, as if this interested her. "Our singers—they're like your tale tellers—they say that long ago, when Sea people walked more on the Land, mixed bloods lived here sometimes. There was a man, Artair, who could shape water. He made it carve pebbles. A woman called Cait shaped water as she sang. I don't know why they chose to do only those things. Or if they could do others. I also don't know how they learned. From living in Asrai and hearing that mixed bloods shaped water, maybe? That's why I assumed you'd learned from your book. Because you wouldn't have heard."

"I see." A heat swelled in Margot, filling, blazing. Even shaping magic made her strange. She'd heard enough for now. "I'll eat and drink later," she said, and gestured to the door. "I'm sure you need to get back."

"It isn't my watch. That's why I came to talk with you. But you're impossible to talk with," said Esyllt, sounding irritated. "I speak and you barely speak back."

"Why would you want to? I'm a cousin with tainted blood," Margot snapped. "A Land Creeper, as you call us."

Esyllt flushed. She pushed back wisps of hair, almost as if suddenly nervous or embarrassed. "I don't call all Land Walkers that. Just the ones ignorant about water." Her voice lowered. "Not all of us feel as the chieftain does about Land Walkers. I don't think you're tainted. Just different."

"Different," Margot said, the blaze still inside her despite the explanation. "I am different everywhere."

The door to the room swung open, and Aerinwy strode in. Behind her, unearthly wails, a keening, came from the hallway. She wore a fur cloak. No, she wore her gray sealskin. Her eyelids and her lips were painted black. They made her look feral. "Margot of Pristanne, you have to make your decision. Orrin of Mawr is searching for you. It's dangerous for us to keep you here." The chieftain held up a chain with a shell locket. "We've already lost a gatekeeper who tried to stop the seeking magic."

"Dennys fell," Esyllt whispered.

"You can join the rest of your order, Esyllt, Gatekeeper," Aerinwy said.

As Esyllt left, Margot stared at the locket. The mourning cries raced around her and through her. Orrin's hands, the lightning magic in them, had done this. The gatekeeper, like Bird, had been hurt by those fingers Margot had loved on her face and bare neck. Other holy men and maybe all of Mawr would cheer that magic on, but she wanted to scrub the places where he'd touched her.

The wailing in the hallway continued, rising and falling. Stepping toward Margot, her eyes hard, the chieftain said, "Go back to him. Pretend to reconcile. Learn when he next travels on the Sea. If I know when to expect him, his boat will sink. Go now. Make amends for your foolishness."

"Foolishness? I didn't choose to give Orrin the book." The shadow laughter twisted through Margot again. She'd come here looking for a home and instead had found one more person who wanted to make use of her.

This wasn't her place. She didn't have a place. She'd leave, belonging to no one and nothing. She'd find the book and take it back. Neither Orrin nor Aerinwy would have the satisfaction of owning it. She didn't know what she'd do after. That was too far away. "I'll tell the storyteller. Then I want to go—"

"Good," interrupted Aerinwy, giving her small, tight smile, misunderstanding. "If the king's sailing soon, we'll wait and find the book after his boat sinks. If he isn't, we'll have to get it away from him quickly. Before it breaks and gives him its secrets."

"That's not what I mean," said Margot. "I'm leaving. You can fight Orrin yourself." Or not. She'd be no part of what they did or didn't do.

Aerinwy's smile disappeared. Her savage face was grim. "What about the book?" she asked.

Margot felt no fear. "If you find it, you'll get it back," she said, her own face, all of her, just as grim. The chieftain wouldn't find it. Margot would take it from Orrin; then she'd decide what to do with it.

"You won't help us? You'll just return to the Land and leave the book to Orrin, until we win it back?" The chieftain made a fist around the locket. Sarcasm honed her voice. "You'll just wander around the coast, or maybe settle with a fisherman who bashes seals when he can because they ruin his nets? I think not. You mean to get the book back for yourself. Ariana Elin shouldn't have made it, or passed it down. You can't have it any longer."

Ariana had passed it down. It was Margot's now; she'd decide its fate. "I have to go," Margot said. The rest was no one's concern but hers. Nothing about her was anyone's concern. "I should start soon."

"You choose Land, then. You could have Sea but choose Land. Think hard. You won't be able to grab the book from Orrin without our help. Even if you do manage, we'll take it from you," Aerinwy said with contempt. "Make this choice, and I'll ban you from Asrai." Her voice was cutting. She meant this to punish, to hurt. "You won't be able to change your mind later. It, and we, will be forever lost to you."

Margot stared at the chieftain, seeing with sharper eyes the seal woman's pale skin, like her own pale skin; the white streaks in straight black hair that she, too, would have when she grew older. She also saw the sealskin she'd never have, and the way the chieftain looked at her, so like the way those in Pristanne had looked at her. These people were already lost to her; they always had been.

"I won't stay here," Margot said. Aerinwy's face was vengeful. She seemed about to turn her back, to dismiss and ignore Margot. Before she could, Margot told her, "Because I choose neither. Not Land. And not Sea."

# Twenty-three

argot walked quickly through the dim corridors of Asrai. Esyllt, whose face was now painted with black like the chieftain's, walked with her. Margot wasn't allowed to go anywhere alone. She also had to stay in these passages they called the outlands. She'd never see more of the Sea people's realm. Esyllt had told her this, not Aerinwy. The chieftain hadn't talked to her again. For Aerinwy, Margot no longer existed. She was like a criminal who was too insignificant to worry about.

Margot's arms and legs were fleet and agile. She felt fiercer than she ever had before. The bragha would arrive within hours. She'd called him, or rather, Esyllt had called him for her. The gatekeeper had stood near the water. She'd opened her mouth as if she were screaming. Margot hadn't heard anything, but the cry was high and loud, Esyllt had said, and he'd hear it. Aerinwy might not think her a threat, but she was. She'd say goodbye to Bird; he was better, she no longer had to look after him. Then, once the bragha arrived, she'd go find a way to get the book first.

The hallway split. Esyllt had been talking but had gone awkwardly silent after mentioning that wisdoms helped to protect Asrai. How they did it was a Sea secret, one Margot wasn't allowed to know. Margot was tired of reminders that she didn't belong. She couldn't leave here soon enough.

She and Esyllt turned into another passage. A sudden breeze rushed by them. The magic in it made Margot's face warm with that sparking-fire feeling. She tried to ignore the breeze, but she had the stray thought that magic roamed wild here—as did the people, most likely. They came, they went and swam the Sea. On land, magic didn't rain down freely. People didn't roam wild. Without realizing it, she'd stretched out her hand. The breeze was rushing past each finger. She made a fist. She wouldn't let herself miss anything about this place.

She and Esyllt went through maze-like corridors. They walked by a gatekeeper with a long curved knife. His face was also painted black, because they were all in mourning, maybe. Behind him walked a woman wearing a broad leather belt studded with twisting shells. Over one shoulder she carried a string of dead creatures with tentacles. Esyllt leaned so close Margot could smell a fragrance in her hair that was surprisingly like wildflowers. Esyllt said, "A merchant, Baez."

As if Margot needed or wanted to learn these people's names. They passed, and she looked to the side instead of at them. It was so dark. "No sunlight," Margot said, "ever." It had felt like night, one endless night, since she'd arrived.

"No," said Esyllt. "On sunny days, we bask on the Land. On the rocks. With winter arriving, we won't go up often." The gatekeeper sounded bleak, as if staying away from the rocks was hard for her to bear.

Margot thought of the nest Esyllt kept and the wildflower scent in her hair. It could be that Esyllt liked the land more than most. Perhaps she even liked it more than Aerinwy would allow. Margot didn't ask. It was no concern of hers.

They finally reached the rooms where Bird was staying. Esyllt stopped. "I'll wait out here until you're done."

"Aren't you supposed to follow me?" Margot asked.

"You came to talk to the storyteller," said Esyllt, stony-faced. "Any of our people would expect and receive privacy."

Esyllt sounded defiant, as if she might be disobeying Aerinwy. Saying thank you didn't seem quite enough. The gate-keeper had answered questions when she could. She'd given Margot a cloak to wrap up in and a pallet to sleep on. Esyllt had been decent to her. Despite this, Margot couldn't think of anything better to say. "Thank you."

"My welcome," Esyllt said with a slight smile. "Cousin."

Margot just nodded. Esyllt was better than the rest, but Margot belonged to no place and no one.

She went through the room with the rolled furs and then back to the small cave room. She found Bird awake, sitting on the pallet. His hair was combed smooth and braided, like hers. He wore a simple long tunic and trousers. His skin was healthier, but he seemed different from the man he'd been before Orrin's magic had touched him. Small lines were at the outer corners of his black eyes. Also, he had an unfamiliar, faraway look that troubled her. He didn't meet her gaze. Instead, he stared out the polished stone at the black water. He was neither the feverish, struggling man he'd been since they'd left land, nor the mischievous voice at her window. She wasn't sure who he was now. "I came to say goodbye. I'm going," she said.

"I was wondering where you were." His voice was as lovely as it had been before, but he still didn't look at her. A part of him seemed far off, as if while walking so close to death he'd left a piece of himself with its gatekeeper. Her worry grew. He added, "I hear the chieftain has kicked you out, Lady."

"Don't call me Lady. I'm Margot, just Margot. Aerinwy

doesn't think much of land people, or people with water in their blood, and I won't do something she wants me to do. So I'm going," Margot answered, expecting him to ask more. He didn't, nor did he say goodbye. "Do you feel all right?"

"I'm better." He gestured at the window. "I've thought of staying longer. The wisdom said they have a kind of respect for storytellers—or singers, as they call theirs. They think it bad luck to offend one. Would that Orrin thought so."

"You don't have to leave when I do," she explained, feeling as if he wasn't quite hearing her. "You can go when you're ready."

"I'll go. Though a storyteller, I'm still a Land Walker. I'd have to stay in these outer passages. Outlands, the places they only travel through, or use sometimes to hide from seal hunters. I wouldn't be good at obeying such a rule." Then he said softly, "I think I found what I had to, anyway. The fisherman's boy. I don't know that I would have without coming here."

"The fisherman's boy?" Margot asked. She lowered herself onto a stone bench, her hands on a stone table. She couldn't really feel either one. He spoke without sense; part of him had gone on to death. She didn't want him trailing after her. She wanted him to make his stories and tell them, though, maybe whisper them at someone else's window. "Who's the fisherman's boy?" she asked.

He looked at her for the first time, surprised. Then he laughed. "I'm sorry. I must sound witless. It's a boy in a story I'm weaving," he said. "The story isn't finished yet, and I've been thinking more of it than anything else."

"One that you're making? You've started it? When can I hear it?" she said, then wanted to take the words back; she'd sounded so eager. She only meant that she was glad he'd still tell tales. She didn't want him to mistake her eagerness for anything else. Rising, she was agile and fierce again. She was ready to get her journey started, to go her way while he went his. "We already called one of the braghas, the creatures that brought us. It might be here soon. You don't have to come with me."

"I'm going now, even if you won't take my help." He studied his hands, smiling. "I might not finish this tale for a long time. But you can hear it when it is finished, if you want." His voice was suddenly ferocious, as if making and telling the tale was what he meant to do, as she meant to find the book. He knew what her ferocity felt like. He added, "When you get back, where do you think you'll live? Where will you go?"

"It's not important," she said brusquely. But the questions seemed to press more than they had before, when they were in the back of her mind. Whether she triumphed or failed, if Orrin didn't kill her or capture her, she'd have to go somewhere. Much as she'd like to see Belinde and tell her about a realm ruled by a woman, she'd never go back to the midlands. She'd find a place by the Sea. It would be a lonely, hidden place, where few lived. Still, she'd need to eat. She wouldn't be able to avoid everyone; there'd be people she served or harvested with, people she traded with. They'd all watch her out of the corners of their eyes. They'd want to know what she knew. "The lands are big. There are plenty of places," she said, crossing her arms over her chest.

"True, but he'll be looking for you, I think." Bird paused, then asked, "Are you all right?"

"Of course," Margot said, dropping her arms. She didn't want to explain.

The bell on the door jangled. A young man with black curls and a belt of strung stones came in with a tray. He set a plate and a pitcher on the table. He stared at the wall beyond Margot instead of at her. His nose wrinkled as if the room stank, and he said, "The gatekeeper on watch sent word to you and Esyllt that the bragha hasn't arrived yet. The waters are still rough and stormy." He didn't wait for any response, just turned and went.

Once Margot left here, she was done with this kind of waiting and feeling trapped. She'd make her own decisions, and go where she wanted, when she wanted.

"He doesn't like us much," Bird said wryly. He rose from his pallet, paced to the hearth and back. "I'm not hungry, and I don't have anything to pack or prepare. Would you like to hear a story? I don't have the strength for a long one, but even a short one would help us pass the time. Unless you have to go to your room. You could wait there instead. Or you could wait here."

"You don't have to tell a story for me. You should probably rest," Margot said. Hearing a tale would make time speed on, but she didn't need him to grant her a favor.

"I don't need to rest. I will tell a tale if you ask me to, though. Or not. I'm at your command. Storytelling does make waiting, and many things, easier." He seemed to be staring at something far off again, but at a more frightening place than the one where his unfinished story lived.

Margot remembered how he'd hung like a sack on the bragha, his breaths shallow and unsteady under her knuckles. She didn't need to hear a story, but he needed to speak one. "Tell something funny," she suggested.

He grinned his usual mischievous grin. Then he was silent, his head tilted as if he were listening. Margot tapped her fingers against her sides, wanting this done, wanting to go. He straightened with a look of relief she didn't understand, and spoke.

*"Gwist was a fool, a king's fool,*
*a liar, a cheat, and a thief.*
*He planned to take the crown from the king's own head,*
*and sell it*
*for a lord's cloak,*
*a pipe,*
*and strong tobacco to enjoy through the winter."*

He raised his hands. Golden liquid light streamed down his arms and swirled around him. It wove into an illusion of the scrawny, clever-eyed Gwist. Margot knew the illusion should be clearer. She shouldn't be able to see Bird, with his braided black hair and blue tunic, through Gwist. It was as if both Bird and Gwist were ghosts, one behind the other. Still, the rich melody of Bird's voice and the glimmering bright illusion made her stare.

As Bird spoke of Gwist's schemes, the illusion spun and changed. It was thinner than parchment, thinner than mist. She could see each round, gleaming droplet of color. They were like a moving mosaic. Like the mosaic of Asrai the bragha had shown her.

Stunned, Margot watched each bright droplet, so like air and water, surface and depth. She could shape such a vision. She could already feel within her the way the water would move. Its pieces would fit into a whole, small alone, but great together. There was water in the room. She could smell its fresh scent. It was in the pitcher that was on the stone table.

Shaping water was not a magic of Land or of Sea. It was one of the things that made her different, a stranger everywhere. But her hand reached. She could have nothing else she wanted, but she could shape a piece of the Sea.

Always before, she'd scooped water. This time it sprang up

at a gesture from her hand, in many droplets. She realized Bird had stopped. His illusion of Gwist was frozen as if trapped in ice. His own face behind the illusion was astonished. "Keep telling the tale," she said, feeling her water droplets, air and water, surface and depth, hovering. It was as if she were hovering, too; she couldn't feel the ground anymore.

Bird started again with a faltering string of words that became a whisper.

*"Gwist came to the queen first, thinking her crown would bring him extra finery."*

Margot heard the whisper and stepped up to her floating water. She stood before it. With quick movements of fingers and palms and fingernails, she pushed the droplets into the shape of a face: a long, slender neck, a gown, a crown. The water became the queen Gwist hoped to trick. The drops shone iridescent at Margot's touch.

Bird walked around her and around the iridescent queen. His illusion of Gwist came with him. They were like two ghosts shining with magic. He stopped opposite Margot, the queen and Gwist between them. *"While the queen talked of cakes and gowns, he took her crown right from her brow,"* he said, his words still a whisper. He reached, Gwist reached, for the water queen's crown. They touched it, running fingers across its bright edge. Margot watched the fingers. She could feel the light and heat of Bird's magic. It made the water it touched, and her, warm and golden.

Gwist faded and disappeared, though Bird still shone with magic. He traced the queen's face. Margot could feel his fingers. There were graceful, like his voice.

He looked from the queen to Margot. Margot forgot to

breathe. He could see her. He could see the joy and wholeness she felt when she shaped water. He could see how utterly different she was. And his eyes were black as the Sea on a moonless night. She wanted to be nearer to those eyes, those hands, that voice. As near as she could get.

Her heart scuttled in her chest.

He couldn't be feeling the same. Not about what he saw of her. Or if he did, he just wanted to own what she was, as Orrin had. She dropped the water with a crash and stepped back from him.

Bird looked shocked. Margot couldn't tell if he thought her tainted or ugly or something to be owned and used. Her heart thudded. She didn't want to know what he thought of her. "I'm sorry I ruined the story. I should've just let you tell it. I shape water." She wasn't able to stop her tongue. "People who have water in their blood can. It's a kind of magic. I've never tried that before. I shouldn't have, not while you were telling a story.

"I'm not ready to leave yet. I have to get my things," she said, although she didn't have any things to get. She left without giving him a chance to respond. She fixed her mind on her book, on taking it away from everyone, burying it, and then disappearing.

# Twenty-four

ird walked up the dim corridor, following the Lady, who said nothing. She'd told him to call her Margot, but he couldn't think of her that way. She went around a corner. He followed. She'd shaped water with a magic he'd never heard mentioned. He couldn't forget the sleek feel of the iridescent queen under his hand. And meeting the Lady's eyes had almost been like touching skin to skin. Then she'd dropped the water, left the room, and stopped talking to him almost completely.

He watched her walk ahead. There could be many reasons why she'd stopped talking. Orrin had hurt her. Neither of them knew where they'd go when they reached land, and they'd both be criminals who'd angered Beloved Orrin. It could be she simply didn't like him much. He was a coward and didn't ask for her reason. He'd rather not know than get an answer he didn't want to hear. So he silently followed.

They went through a door onto a dark ledge. The Sea was held back by some invisible barrier. The lights on the ledge glowed eerily. Standing there was a woman whose face was so like the Lady's they could have been sisters. She was by two white lights shaped like seals, the braghas. Bird had a glimpse of his fisherman's boy on this ledge. The boy would see as little as others in stories did: just rock, a woman with seal eyes, dark empty passages, and dim rooms. His sly laughter would echo against the barrier and rock. The Lady glanced his way and the glimpse of the boy was gone. Heat flashed in Bird. She said nothing. Neither did he.

The woman, Esyllt, told Bird how he'd have to ride the bragha to the surface. "You're certain you want to go?" the creature nearest the Lady asked her in a gravelly voice.

The Lady seemed suddenly irritated. "I'm sure. I came. Now I want to go back."

The bragha gave what looked like an exasperated head toss. "If that's what you want." It sounded dismissive. "You won't stay and learn more of your people? That's why Ariana Elin wanted me to answer the call and bring you, any of her descendants, here."

"They aren't *my* people," the Lady said. Bird could hear her hurt and hardness. He wanted to know more about what this all meant.

"I won't bring you back," the creature replied, its voice just as hard but without the hurt. "And you lost the thing that would call me for any others of your line."

The Lady and the Sea woman's faces became mirrors for each other. They were both pinched and grave. Bird could see "the thing" was important to them. He wanted to know more about that, also.

The women didn't explain, though. The Lady said thanks and goodbye to Esyllt, her tone softer and awkward. Then she climbed on her now silent bragha. Bird lowered himself, with respect, onto his. Its skin was as smooth as any seal's. They plunged into the chilly Sea.

The trip was like a dream full of rushing water and breathlessness. Long before they reached the surface, Bird felt feverish and knew he wasn't wholly recovered from Orrin's magic. He closed his eyes and held on. He thought his lungs would burst. Then he was surrounded by a wind that blew cold. The storm that had started as they'd left was still raging, or a new one had blown in. Sharp, bitter rain beat down.

The bragha was a horse beneath Bird, running as if the water were land. Bird wanted a bed and a fire. He'd settle for a half-dry cave. The journey went on and on. The Lady's bragha veered. She was leaning over its neck, directing it. Maybe she knew of a cave. Or she knew a place she wanted to leave him. Bird breathed on his frozen fingers rather than asking.

They reached rocks and sand, a cove. The bragha melted from beneath them. The Lady's dived away. Bird's said, "Farewell, Tale Teller." The sound of the scraping voice faded from his head. Then he realized he and the Lady were together on the shore. She hadn't left him. But he couldn't think why, of all places, she'd brought them here.

The castle sat above them and to their left, on the cliff. Beside it, the garden's trees lashed in the wind. The cliffs before them had openings like small mouths. He and the Lady had to get to them without Orrin's seeing. "Where should we go?" Bird asked, then fell silent. The Lady stared up at the heart's wood and blackspine trees as if she hadn't heard him. "Are you hurt?" he asked. Her look was shocked. It made the hair on his arms prickle. "What's wrong?"

"He hid things in the heart's wood tree as a boy. That's it. That's where it is." She started to climb the rocks out of the cove. She seemed entirely unaware that anyone might see her.

"Are you mad?" Bird asked, but not loud enough for her to hear. "Wait," he said, catching up to her. His feverish aching sank. "Why go now?"

"He's trying to steal what's in it." She sounded as savage as he felt about the stories Orrin's magic had ruined. "The Sea people are searching for it, too. They'll keep it if they find it. It's mine, passed down to me, and now I know where it is."

She'd come here because of the thing she'd lost, the thing that could call the bragha. Orrin had taken it. She meant to get it back. Did she want his help? "There are other steps," he said. "There's a stairway that leads up the cliff. It'll bring you to the other side of the garden, opposite the gate. No one will be on it, not in this storm." He pointed farther down the shore. She didn't say goodbye, just started off.

He trailed after her. She didn't stop him. The choice to follow or not seemed to be his. He rubbed his prickling arms. If she was quick, she'd be gone before anyone suspected. The Lady would outwit Beloved Orrin. Bird smiled. This route would be dangerous, but he'd take it for now.

The steps up the cliff were slippery and crumbling. She climbed them two at a time. He followed. Words began to wing inside him. They weren't strays, however, wholly unconnected: *Stone. Slick. Chill. The sky wailed.*

At the top of the steps, the Lady went through a maze of boulders until she reached the garden wall. They saw no swordsmen. She scrambled up the wall, crushing and dislodging creeping vines as she went. Rain and wind pushed at Bird. He remembered the taste of Orrin's metallic magic on his tongue. *Silent*, the words murmured. *Quick.*

The Lady jumped from the top of the wall into the garden. Bird was up and then over. He stumbled. The memory of the metallic taste bit into him. He remembered the hurt. He heard his words' whispering: *Dusk. Stealthy.* The memories drew back. He kept going.

The Lady led the way through squat raspian. They went past blackspine, sweet oak, and heart's wood. She stopped by a heart's wood tree with a bench beneath it. It was thick and gnarled with long, arching boughs. The wind was making it creak and sway. "Stop," she said to him. "Don't come too close. Leave me room." They'd reached what they had to.

Her voice trailed away. She walked around the tree. She was staring at it as if she might read some hidden message among its few remaining leaves. Even with the wind beating at him, Bird caught a scent. He'd smelled it in his sickroom before the Lady had made the water rise. It was the scent of her unfamiliar water magic, and it reminded him of the Sea wind in the early morning. As before, she didn't seem to notice it. She reached for the tree trunk. Even in the growing dimness, she looked clear-eyed and ferocious. Bird no longer cared that exhaustion was making both his arms tremble. *Glorious.* This word rang louder within him than all the rest. Whatever happened here would be glorious.

The Lady had one hand on the tree's trunk. The smell of the early-morning Sea grew. Then lightning burst from the tree's bark, and suddenly the stench of Orrin's magic made Bird cough. It poured around the Lady's hand, enfolded it, and began to move up her arm. She coughed, too. She pulled back, but the lightning wrapped around her. Alarmed, Bird stepped toward her.

The Lady pushed at the lightning as if it were a solid thing, a hand groping for her. Then she stopped fighting it and walked into it, toward the tree. It sped around her arms and chest and head. Bird went forward, meaning to yank her out, then stopped. Lit up, she was intent. The moment seemed still, ready to tip for her or against her. *Glory* or *Loss.* He wouldn't be the cause of its falling the wrong way. He waited, his breaths shallow.

The smell of the Lady's water magic broke through the lightning. The lightning shredded and fell away from her. In the channels of the tree's rough bark, rivulets of silver glinted and coursed. Their brightness made the lightning dim, then fade. The tree's sap, Bird realized, so like water, was heeding the Lady's magic. The bark ran with silver, all up the trunk and branches, even into the last leaves. The tree and the Lady were bathed in the silver light. Bird stood transfixed.

The glinting silver ran bright all around the Lady's hand. She grinned, and cast an exultant glance toward him. Then she looked back at the trunk. As the last lightning cleared, the silver faded, except the bright circle around the Lady's hand. The Lady pulled the circle; it opened like a door. She lifted something from the opening: a book.

Then Bird's head filled with a ghost of screaming pain. It made him recoil inside. He saw Orrin striding toward them without any cloak, his yellow hair plastered around his face. His raised hands were wreathed in lightning. Bird called to the Lady, "Run."

She went forward instead. In Orrin's direction. She was walking to meet him. "Stop it," she told Orrin. It was as if she hadn't heard Bird, or didn't remember he was there.

Bird was rooted where he stood. Seeing Orrin, facing Orrin, was more important to the Lady than escaping. She *wanted* to see him. Bird had the petty, dangerous urge to step between them. To not let them near each other.

Orrin was close now. His hands flashed. The storm became a gale. It shoved Bird. It scraped his skin raw. Lightning flared. Bird darted behind one of the trees. The lightning seared past, then was gone. He was still here. It hadn't hit him.

"I said stop," the Lady repeated. Orrin drew near to her. They were talking. Bird couldn't hear what they were saying.

He crouched, his legs shaking with fatigue. The storm beat down on him. If he didn't flee, he wouldn't finish his tale of the fisherman's boy; he wouldn't save the stories of his line and pass them to an apprentice; he'd fail his father. The Lady chose to fight with Orrin, not to run with Bird.

He held on to the creaking tree. So he should just slink away? That wouldn't be a story he'd ever want to tell.

She might not care for him at all. He'd stay anyway. He'd help her, if he could. This was the tale of himself he would shape. Though no one might ever hear it.

\~◎\~

Orrin swept one bright hand upward and made the storm pull back, but just from the two of them. Every surface of Margot's skin was alive. She'd grabbed the book—its wild Sea scent and worn leather—from where Orrin had kept it. Now she'd decide where to hide and abandon it.

Orrin was staring at her as if he wanted to yell and throw something, maybe her. His wet face was full of righteous anger, which enraged her. He hadn't even brought Meynard or a swordsman to help. He'd thought getting the book back from her would be easy. He was wrong.

They glared at each other. The storm howled beyond the circle of calm. Bird was out there somewhere. She hadn't meant to bring him. She'd seen where the book was and had come for it; he'd followed. She wished she were sure he was safely away and no longer any of her concern, but she couldn't think too much about him now. Orrin wasn't thinking of Bird. He stared bitterly at her, and she stared bitterly back. She waited to see what he'd say about what she'd done. "Hand me the book," he said, as if she had no other choice.

She had other choices. He wouldn't have the book, its worn spine and pages. No one would. "I have an offer for you." She'd use the book to bargain for her escape, and Bird's, if he needed her help, but she wouldn't really give it to Orrin. She'd bury it where he'd never find it.

"What kind?" he asked severely, but a gale suddenly struck at Margot, and she yelled, "Orrin, stop it!"

Then she saw that he, too, was knocked sideways by the gale, as if caught unprepared. At the edge of the calmness, a woman wearing a gray cloak and trousers held a long, curved knife. She wore black paint around her eyes and on her lips. Esyllt. Behind her, a narrow opening in the calmness closed. The gale was shut out again. "Margot of Pristanne," Esyllt said, her face as savage as Aerinwy's had been.

"You came after me?" Margot demanded. "You think I'll hand the book over to you?"

Esyllt turned to Orrin. "I followed to offer you help, Cousin."

"Who is this?" Orrin demanded. He raised his hands again, magic flaring in them. He seemed ready to loose it. "What cousin?"

"That's not for you to know," Esyllt said, her tone cold.

"I don't need help, Esyllt," Margot snapped. "I won't give the book to you."

Esyllt nodded once. Despite the black paint, she looked younger suddenly, and afraid. "I won't ask you to."

Margot didn't know how to answer. Esyllt was a gatekeeper, and her chieftain wanted the book. Had she gone against Aerinwy? Was Aerinwy somewhere near, out in the storm?

Orrin stepped closer to Margot. "Do you really mean to do this? To insist on taking the book? To defy me and try to leave? You know more about me than anyone ever has." He sounded both furious and pleading. He gestured to the tree where she'd found the book. "You have this power. I felt it break my spells to reach the book." His hands were still lit up, but he held them open before her. "You overstep with it. You don't know anything about magic, its rules and dangers. Yet you can still use it. If you submit it to my control, I could guide it. Then it would be used rightly."

Margot couldn't look away from his blue, blue eyes, the face she used to like so much. He really thought she might submit herself wholly to him.

"Mawr is safe," he continued. "People are happy. The worst stories, the kind that tempt many to disobey or do harm, are silent and will be forgotten. Storytellers will no longer make fun of their betters. The swordsmen keep the roads clear of wanderers; only people with good reason now travel. Lords will always know where their people are. We're learning more about our magic and how it can protect us. Our pure magic will one day force all the demon spirits to stay in their underground kingdom." His eyes showed warring emotions, fury and longing, as he whispered, "You made a mistake with the storyteller, and I should condemn you forever. I can't. Give the book to me, and tell me all you know of it. You must. With your help, I can better study it and use it to learn more of the Sea's secrets. I can make Mawr safer, its holy men wiser. It will be a land like no other."

Mawr would be a land like no other, but would it be better? She wasn't sure. Besides that, he was saying she should pay all the cost, while he got all the benefit. This is what he truly believed. She wanted him to know cost.

The book's Sea smell was in her nose. She could feel other eyes on her. Esyllt was watching, and maybe from somewhere out in the storm, Bird. Orrin was waiting for her answer, poised, magic-bright hands open. She held the book tighter. He would hurt, and she would laugh.

She rubbed her thumbs against the cover's edges, preparing to tell Orrin he couldn't have what he wanted. Then she stopped, looking down. She'd thought . . . She had to be mistaken. Her hands loosened. She held the book with her fingertips, really feeling.

She felt the cover, the surface. And she felt a tension, water meeting air.

Beads of Sea water, as small as a baby's tears, made up the cover. She could feel how they came together, their sides barely pressing. As when she shaped water, the drops sat on others below, shifting slightly in their places. She didn't need to open the book. She could feel how the water made pages, letters, and familiar words. She could feel the way it formed pictures and the map. Deeper, in hidden corners, were unfamiliar shapes. There were magics and words she hadn't found yet in the book. Slowly, carefully, her fingers moved. They caressed the drops that made the title. The letters rippled. A pounding, a thrilled beating was in her ears. It was the beat of her heart.

"Margot?" Orrin's forehead was creased. He sounded wary. "What's wrong?"

Her heart beat like waves on the shore. The book was made of water. She pressed her palm against its cover. It still looked like leather, but she felt the slight rounding of each bead. They were shaped to have form, scent, and texture. The book kept its form, and it had places to hide secrets. Though not a mixed blood, Ariana Elin had somehow made this.

It had led her, misled her, to Asrai. She meant to hide it from everyone. She meant to bury it and leave it behind, to use it to lash back at Orrin.

But she might learn from it to shape scent and texture. Her heart made her chest hurt.

"I won't give it up."

Margot realized she'd spoken aloud. Orrin jerked back from her as if shoved; he'd actually thought she'd go back to him. Her pleasure at his hurt was fainter than she'd thought it would be. She ran one finger against the page's edges. They were shaped water, every single one. "I have no place with you."

Orrin straightened, one hand raised menacingly. Esyllt thrust her knife between Orrin and Margot as if that might protect her. "Then I'll take it," Orrin said, his hands shining. The storm poured into the circle, shrieking in Margot's ears. Esyllt dropped to her knees, her knife glowing but not seeming to help her. The magic had an awful metallic stench. It didn't stink of demon spirits. It was holy-man magic—pure magic, Orrin had said, magic that protected Mawr. Despite that, fear stabbed Margot hard. Orrin would use this magic to hurt them all badly. They had to get away.

"Run," Margot shouted to Esyllt, and to Bird, though he might have already left or fallen. The wind ripped her words away. The magic's stink made her gag. Branches broke and whirled by her. Lighting flashed all around. Suddenly, Esyllt seemed to be gone or struck down. Margot hugged *The Book of the Sea*. Orrin's hands were on the cover. They pulled and the book slipped. Orrin stood steady, unaffected by the storm, and didn't look at Margot's face. He'd call his magic good; it seemed to her no better than the spirits'. He'd use it to take her book's secrets. He'd give Bird's voice, Esyllt, and her to the storm.

"No," Margot cried, and reached.

She reached for the feel of water. She felt her book. She

reached beyond, down through the earth beneath her feet. Water soaked into soil. It rested in land. She was this water, raging, rising.

A river rose from the soil. It licked her boots. She was confused for a moment. What were boots? The smallest of voices reminded her that she was Margot. She was merely calling water, she was not made of water. But then she was the river again.

It swelled straight from the land and grasped the man, Orrin. It dragged him through the garden and over the wall. The river ran down the cliff, breaking and rejoining as it sped around poor, earthbound stone. Sea waves reached out beyond the boundary of tide. They rushed up the sand and rock. They took the man and his lightning magic into their green-blue depths and their early-winter cold, all the bad-tasting flash of them. The man, Orrin, cursed and cried as they pulled him away from the shore.

River became part of Sea. But there was a piece that didn't melt from fresh water into salt water. It had bones, a body. The body still crouched in the garden. It was not Sea, but Margot.

Her legs and arms were like lead, shivering lead. Her spine was too weak to hold her straight. Margot lowered herself and lay on the ground, drawing her arms and legs to her chest.

The rain pounded on a dry garden, a desert of sand and dried-out skeletons of trees. All the water was gone except the wet remnants of a path running over the wall and toward the Sea. The trees would die, if they weren't dead already. She listened to the murmuring Sea far below. She moved aching fingers and blinked aching eyes. She missed the rising and rushing.

Still, her arms and body were wrapped around water. It was the length and width of one hand span, shaped into a leather cover, vellum pages, letters with odd twists and curls, and many other things she had yet to learn. She closed her eyes and rested her hand on it.

She was different, landless, placeless.

She shaped water. She had a book shaped of water. That was her land and her place.

# Twenty-five

rousers rolled up, Bird waded in the shallow, rocky pool. His feet were numb. He didn't climb onto the rocks.

Watchful, he looked across the gray water. Swordsmen would be searching for them, as would Aerinwy. Night would come soon. The others would be at the small sturdy shack, preparing to leave.

The shack belonged to a broad, often silent man. The man belonged to Esyllt. The Lady had found out she'd been disobeying her chieftain for months, coming to see this man on his remote rock of an island. Now she'd left the chieftain because she'd chosen to help the Lady. Also because, Bird thought, once she'd met this man, she'd always meant to leave Asrai.

Bird looked back at the smoke coming from the smoke hole in the gray shack's roof. This island belonged to Mawr, in name, anyway, but the man didn't care for kings and swordsmen. He went to nearby villages and to Syllig to trade for what he couldn't grow, make, or catch. He had an old wall to keep the now rare demon spirits away. He traded with the holy men so that they'd mend it when mending was needed. Bird had slept for a full day and night, like the rest, and had been too weary to tell stories, but the man had said he liked Gwist tales best. Hearing the man say this had almost made Bird cry.

Bird pushed at the water with his feet. He hadn't needed to help the Lady in the castle garden. With her dazzling magic, she'd dragged Orrin out to Sea. All the same, she'd said Orrin would still be able to reach the land. That meant Bird couldn't go back to Sharp Maud, Syllig, his father's grave, or his mother's house. He'd have to travel and hide. But there were people, like Sharp Maud and this man, Douglas, who'd want to hear forbidden tales. He'd find those people and keep the stories alive.

He sat on a larger rock, pulling his feet from the cold water. And what about the Lady?

He'd thought of slipping away. That was all he'd done: thought. Instead, he'd lingered. He'd listened for her to ask him to join her. He was spineless.

Without illusions, he began to line up words like pebbles for his fisherman's boy: *Narrow. Boat. Rain. Night. Riddles.* His story was growing. His father would have liked it.

He should go.

He sat with his words, not going.

∼⟨ℰ⟩∽

Still weary, Margot followed Esyllt into the mud-and-daub hen house. Esyllt pushed one flustered hen from her roost with a practiced hand. Margot wanted to ask, *Why have you left the Sea?* As much as Esyllt loved the land, she would never really belong on it. And if she had children, they wouldn't belong anywhere. Esyllt didn't seem to understand what that would be like. "You're sure you won't stay here?" Margot asked. "I can go alone." She was touched that Esyllt wanted to join her, but she didn't want to see her cousin have mixed-blood children or regret her choice.

"The chieftain will try to find both of us. Orrin will look for you once he reaches land," Esyllt said. Her brown eyes were a little too wide, as if she couldn't believe where she was. "You have no dagger. You need someone to teach you to fight. Traveling alone will quickly attract demon spirits. You haven't spent your life fighting them, as I have. Douglas will take us up the coast toward the Far North. No one knows all the caves and inlets like he does. Also, no one will expect us to go north in autumn and winter." Esyllt still had too wide eyes, but she smiled. "Or maybe I need you to protect me."

Margot saw in her mind's eye trees dried to dead wood and earth turned to sand. Triumph and nausea circled slowly in her stomach. She'd saved her book and herself, but she could have drowned Orrin the way she'd killed the trees. She had the strength. That was part of who she was.

As they finished with the hens, Margot saw Esyllt cup one of the still-warm eggs. She rubbed it against her cheek. Margot looked at the mud wall instead of her cousin. They'd go together. But only for as long as Esyllt preferred warm eggs and Douglas to Asrai.

Esyllt returned to the shack. Though Margot was tired, she didn't go with her. There was still the problem of Bird. He was out here somewhere, unless he'd decided to disappear. He'd listened to their plans but he hadn't demanded to come with them. He hadn't really said anything. She began to walk slowly over the rocks, lichen, and stalky grasses. If he'd disappeared, then there'd be no stories, no chance he might want to use her, no golden touches on her face, and no explanations. He'd just be gone, and she wouldn't have to think of him anymore.

The wind blew her hair. The sack hanging from her shoulders was heavy. One hand reached back. She felt a corner of her book through the wool. It had pictures again. Some were the same as before. Others were different, and she suspected Aerinwy had been right to fear it would tell her more of Sea people and Ariana Elin, as well as other secrets. This morning, before anyone was awake, she'd used the smallest trickle of magic. Under *Maira Alys of Isles of Pristanne,* she'd made the drops blacken and shape her name: *Margot Adele.* As she'd done so, she'd realized her mother had shaped water to put down her name and the notes about Pristanne's rivers and lakes. Margot had brushed all the names and made them ripple. Because of these women, like them, she'd have to wander and hide. Because of them, like them, she had the book and could shape water.

She kept walking, seeing no one, looking out at the Sea. It was ahead of her, full of high troughs and deep valleys. She ached inside. Neither the Sea nor the land had a home for her, but without both she wouldn't be what she was.

She headed toward a rocky beach, then saw Bird on a flat stretch by the water. He hadn't disappeared. He was kicking his legs over his head like a jester, trying to take steps with his hands, tumbling over. Wishing him gone hadn't made him go.

Staring at him, Margot felt like a coward. Liking him was dangerous. And so was a strength that could drag a man out to Sea. So was wandering, rather than being a tainted daughter or a useful wife or the only mixed blood living in Asrai. Not finding out for certain what Bird might want or do seemed a shrinking into what was easy. As staying with her father, Orrin, or Aerinwy would have been. Margot thought of Belinde shaking her head, exasperated at her stepdaughter's cowardice.

Margot walked over and squatted near Bird, on a rock. He stopped trying to hand-walk. "It's almost night," she said. She picked at a ragged fingernail. She was afraid; she should stand and leave. "What will you do next?"

"I'll tell stories, hide. I'll sneak and skulk." He grinned, but didn't even glance her way. Then he went on, "I'll say this straight out. You're free to say no. I'd travel with you awhile, if you'd let me."

She folded her hands on her knees. He wanted to travel with her. "Would you tell me a story?" she asked. This wasn't an answer; she didn't have one.

He sat and leaned back on his elbows, but looked intently at the Sea, not at her. "If you'd like," he said. He sounded cautious, as if not sure why she'd asked.

"What will you tell?" she asked. She could keep going, just pretend he hadn't asked and she didn't have to answer.

"Whatever you choose," he said simply.

*Whatever you choose.* She'd almost never heard that. The sack and the book were against her damp back. She could hear the easier response in her head. Instead, she asked, "What if I said leave? Would you accept my choice?"

He looked at her straight on. As when they'd been in Asrai, he seemed to see right down to the bottom of her. She wanted to be as near as she could get to him. She wanted to run.

"If you don't want me with you, I'll leave," he said. Then his mouth twitched, as if he couldn't quite stop himself from adding, "Though I had considered stopping the story before its end. You'd have to invite me along so you could hear the rest tomorrow."

A laugh burst out of her. He could be lying or deceiving himself about leaving, but he wasn't lying about the story. "We'll see how well you tell the tale, then," she answered, half serious and half teasing, as he'd been.

He gave a loud, free laugh, still looking at her, still dangerous. She might kiss the mischief on his lips. She might go her own way. Maybe in the end, she'd do both. Regardless, she'd shape her future and every piece of her life the way she shaped water, without shrinking.

# AUTHOR'S NOTE

$\mathcal{T}$he story of Margot's great-grandmother, Ariana Elin, is based on the most well known seal-person—selchie, selkie, silkie—tale. In it, a land man takes a seal woman's skin. He hides the skin and marries her. They have children. She always longs for the water. Eventually, she finds her skin. She returns to the sea and her family there. Sometimes she watches over her land family from the water. This story is often called "The Goodman of Wastness." Some children's authors have retold it, including Susan Cooper in *The Selkie Girl* and Franny Billingsley in *The Folk Keeper*.

There are many other seal tales. *The People of the Sea* by David Thomson has seal stories from the Hebrides, the coasts of Scotland and Ireland, and the Shetland and Orkney Islands. Duncan Williamson, a Scottish traveler and storyteller, wrote a few books for children: *The Tales of the Seal People; The Broonie, Silkies and Fairies;* and *Fireside Tales of Traveller Children.* All of these also have stories of seal people, or silkies, as he called them.

Another place to find folktales or other information about seal people is Orkneyjar (www.orkneyjar.com). This website is devoted to providing information about the land, people, and traditions of Orkney. The folktales I read in these places inspired my creation of Asrai. (This word *Asrai* comes from English folklore. It's the name of a kind of English water fairy.) They also inspired the story Bird tells in the inn, "Sharp Maud and the Seal Woman."

The other stories in this book come from a variety of places. The first tale Margot hears, "Rosalind and the Pig's Head," is a partial retelling of "Osin in Tir na n-Og," which can be found in Jeremiah Curtin's *Myths and Folk Tales of Ireland*. The story Bird hates to tell, "The Good King," is like many folktales with heroes who have exceptional powers as children. "The Lad and the Giant," which Margot loves and Orrin condemns, is similar to "Jack and the Beanstalk," as well as the Norwegian Ash Lad stories. Gwist, one of Bird's favorite characters, is my own invention. He's based on the tricksters that are found in many different kinds of folktales, such as Anansi, Brer Rabbit, Coyote, Loki, and Puck.